Praise for *New York Times* Bestselling Author

Jeanne Ray's

Warm and Wonderful Novels

Julie and Romeo Get Lucky

"Comic and insightful, Ray's latest is a delightful tale of extended family and the inner workings of relationships. Its irresistible charm and romance-at-any-age plot are certain to appeal to women of all ages."

—*Romantic Times*

"This book has all the elements of a best seller—great writing and impossible to stop reading."

—Talk of the Town

"*Julie and Romeo* is one of my favorite books ever, so I was really looking forward to this sequel and I'm happy to say it did not disappoint."

—Bookbitch.com

"Winsome, offbeat . . . it's a corker."

—*The Herald Carolina*

Julie and Romeo

"A captivating romp . . ."

—*People*

"Beguiling."

—*Publishers Weekly*

"Ray uses Shakespeare as a scaffold but frames her tale in her own charming way. . . . The Bard would smile."

—*Houston Chronicle*

"A charming, smart love story with interesting characters and great laughs."

—*The Christian Science Monitor*

"Deliciously witty and wickedly sexy . . . [a] thoroughly modern love story for all ages."

—*The Stuart News/Port St. Lucie News (FL)*

"Original."

—*The New York Times Book Review*

"Smart."

—*Entertainment Weekly*

"All the elements of a great summer read."

—*Boston Herald*

"Entertaining."

—*The Evening Standard* (London)

Step-Ball-Change

"Smart, charming, and funny."

—*Chicago Tribune*

"[A] surefooted charmer. . . . Readers are bound to demand an encore."

—*Boston Herald*

"Funny, believable, and full of surprises, this novel, like time with a good friend, is over far too soon."

—*Library Journal*

"Snappy. . . An endearing narrator, realistic and self-deprecating . . . [Ray] has a gift for lively dialogue that makes the characters snap into place."

—*Publishers Weekly*

"A novel as comfortable and inviting as coffee at your best friend's kitchen table."

—*Booklist*

Eat Cake

"Ray's dialogue is ripe with practical wisdom . . . and her style is warm and lightly funny. . . . She has a proven talent for everyday dramas of family life, and her latest is as toothsome as its predecessors."

—*Publishers Weekly*

Julie and Romeo Get Lucky

Jeanne Ray

POCKET BOOKS

NEW YORK   LONDON   TORONTO   SYDNEY

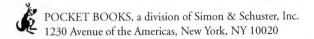
POCKET BOOKS, a division of Simon & Schuster, Inc.
1230 Avenue of the Americas, New York, NY 10020

ISBN-13: 978-1-4165-0969-1
ISBN-10:   1-4165-0969-0
ISBN-13: 978-1-4165-0970-7 (Pbk)
ISBN-10:   1-4165-0970-4 (Pbk)

This Pocket Books trade paperback edition May 2006

10   9   8   7   6   5   4   3   2   1

POCKET and colophon are registered trademarks of
Simon & Schuster, Inc.

Manufactured in the United States of America

Designed by Jaime Putorti

For information regarding special discounts for bulk purchases,
please contact Simon & Schuster Special Sales at 1-800-456-6798 or
business@simonandschuster.com

For Our Grandchildren:

Jeremy Maxwell
Brendan Nancarrow
Lauren Nancarrow
Ben Nash
Emery Nash
Leah Maxwell Pate
Adam Ray
Ashley Ray
James Ray
Jossy Ray

And our great grandchild:

Audrey Pate

We continue to learn from you.

"Fortune brings in some boats
that are not steered."
—William Shakespeare

Chapter One

I HEARD THE CANDYMAN'S VOICE AS SOON AS I opened the door.

"Who can make the sun shine?" he asked.

Romeo leaned in close to me, whispered against the back of my neck, "He's in there."

It was October in Somerville, Massachusetts, and fall was whipping around us with flat orange leaves cutting through the cool orange light of late afternoon. I was going into my house with the man that I loved, that man I was too old to call my boyfriend and too square to call my lover. The man I thought of always as my good fortune, Romeo.

But the Candyman stopped me cold. It was a visceral reaction. Every time I heard him, I wanted to run screaming down the street.

"Sprinkle it with dew," the Candyman sang.

I closed my eyes and panted a little, a technique I used to help quell nausea. The thought of all that candy—which had seemed like such a charming childhood fantasy, when I first saw the movie in 1971—now left me feeling like a six-year-old at ten o'clock on Halloween night. But it wasn't just the candy, it was the movie itself: the insipid singing, the cheesy sets, the tired diatribe of rich and poor and good and evil. Even Willie Wonka, who had once seemed so charming in all his twinkling subversiveness, now made me queasy—because anyone will make you queasy after you watch him eat a teacup for the sixth thousandth time. According to my sloppy calculations, that was approximately how many times my granddaughter Sarah had watched *Willie Wonka and the Chocolate Factory* in my house.

Oh sure, she'd been stuck on other movies before this. It had started out with *Barney's Big Adventure,* then progressed through *Mary Poppins* and *The Little Mermaid,* but those she only watched often, not constantly. Since the Christmas before last, when I so foolishly brought the plague of chocolate into our lives all wrapped up in red Santa paper, there had not been a day that she hadn't played the videotape.

If my mother could rise up from her grave to carp at me, she would say it was my own fault. "What business do Jews have giving Christmas presents in the first place?" she would say to me and shake her head in disgust.

And maybe she would be right. Maybe this was all a curse I brought down on myself. The video followed us like a debt, an insidious disease. There had not been a moment's respite, not even on the day that Sarah's mother, my daughter Sandy, had reached her absolute limit and yanked it out of the VCR and stepped on it again and again with the heel of her boot. Or that other day six months later when I completely snapped and pulled the tape from its casing, spooling out the celluloid like birthday ribbon. On both of those occasions we ended up racing to the video store with a wailing, hyperventilating child in our arms, as frantic as any family stumbling into the emergency room with a blue baby.

We discussed the possibility of seeing a family counselor or staging an intervention. We had been told by countless dispensers of free advice that Sarah would give up the tape as soon as we no longer responded to it, and so we trained ourselves not to respond, or to respond only behind a locked bathroom door with our faces pressed into a stack of towels.

I now repeated my mantra to myself: "It is just a noise like any other noise. It is just a noise like any other noise."

"Cover it with chocolate and collect up all the cream," Romeo sang with the Candyman, swaying me back and forth in a samba. Romeo, unlike his duet partner, had a nice voice. I told him to shut up.

"Have a sense of humor," he said. "It's a movie."

"It isn't a *movie*," I told him. "It's a dangerous, deadly device designed by children so that they can rule the world."

Romeo didn't live with me and therefore could not possibly understand. He thought that just because Sarah and her brother Tony sometimes spent the night at his house and she played the tape on his VCR, that meant he knew the score. But no one could understand it unless they had lived through it. Orwell and Kafka had nothing on an eight-year-old's obsession.

Cautiously, we peered past the entry hall. "Hello!" I called out. "Tony, Tony, Sarah, Sandy, we're home!" But the only living thing to amble into the room was Sarah's cat, a fat-faced orange tabby who purred and knocked against my shins. "Oompah-Loompah," I asked, "where is everybody?"

"Everything he bakes, satisfying and delicious," the Candyman replied.

We walked into the living room to see the thin man with Brilliantined hair on TV fling a fistful of butterscotch discs down onto the heads of little children, who scrambled like wolverines to get their share. He dispensed his licorice whips and egg creams even though no one was here watching him. Even Oompah-Loompah recoiled from the sugared carnage and left the room.

"Hello?" Romeo called, although no one appeared to be home.

I picked up the remote from the coffee table, aimed it at all the greedy children on television, and gave the OFF button a decisive stab. The sound that replaced that singing was crystalline, a silence as sweet and clear as a glacial lake. Had there been a glass of champagne at hand, it would have been quiet enough to hear the bubbles burst.

"Oh," I said, taking Romeo in my arms. "Will you listen to that?"

"What?" he said.

"Exactly."

He kissed me. "Where are they?"

"Do we care?" I kissed him back.

He nodded. "We care passionately."

We had not come home for any sort of funny business. We had come home because there was an extra case of gift cards stored in the hall closet, and we were almost out of them at our flower shops. Romeo had offered to come along because he wanted to pick up a new battery pack for the Dust-Buster.

But when you live in a house full of beloved family members, there is no aphrodisiac as potent or immediate as privacy. Youth is all about finding an opportunity to be alone with the person you want to be alone with, and once you are, you get pregnant, and from that moment on you're never alone again.

Romeo and I were sixty-three. Between us we had two houses, two flower shops, eight children, and ten grandchildren. He made me feel sixteen again, but a big part of that was our never-ending quest to sneak off somewhere.

He pulled back, kissed my nose, looked over my shoulder. "Go check the kitchen."

Part of what makes being sixteen so sexy is the stolen moment, sneaking around. *Look! Mom and Dad aren't home! How much time do you think we have?* For us, Mom and Dad had been replaced by our own children.

There was a piece of paper on the kitchen sink, with big letters written in black Magic Marker.

> *Sneaker sale at Filene's. Be back soon.*
> *xxoo, Sandy*

I held it over my head like the last find in a scavenger hunt. "God bless Sandy."

Romeo looked at the paper and smiled. "She leaves you

notes. That's sweet. My boys could move to Tokyo and they wouldn't leave me a note."

"When she was a little kid, she'd leave me a note if she went to the bathroom." I wrapped my arms around his waist and buried my nose, still cold from the October wind, unabashedly into the side of his neck.

"But how do we know how soon soon will be?"

"We have plenty of time. Look," I said, holding up my wristwatch as if it were proof. "It's four-thirty now. Traffic will be at a standstill, and they couldn't have left more than ten minutes ago."

Romeo looked at the note again. "It doesn't say what time they left."

And here I smiled because finally, finally, that damn video was going to play to my advantage. "The Candyman song comes in the first fifteen minutes of the movie. If we piece the story together from the evidence on hand, I'd say Sarah turned the movie on at four-fifteen, and Sandy started to crack at the opening credits. She then told the kids she'd take them shopping. They must have left the house so fast they forgot to turn the television off."

Sarah never allowed herself to watch her favorite parts out of sequence, nor did she allow herself to skip past the parts that even she found excruciatingly boring, like Charlie's mother leaning in the miserable doorframe of the dismal alley where she boiled other people's filthy clothes for a few pennies and sang a song about how her son should keep dreaming.

Romeo put one hand on either side of my head. His eyes were brimming with love. "You're a genius."

"But what about Big Tony?" I glanced furtively at the ceiling above, as if he might be upstairs.

Big Tony, who was not an especially large man, was Romeo's son, as opposed to Little Tony, a very tall, gangly twelve-year-old, who was my grandson. Big Tony was married to my daughter Sandy, and all of them—daughter, son-in-law, and the two children from Sandy's first marriage—lived with me.

Tony and Sandy's marriage meant that Romeo and I were in-laws. I should point out that our love was not a crime against society or nature. There were are no laws in any state prohibiting the commingling of in-laws.

"Tony's in class. I know it because I dropped him off this afternoon," Romeo said.

Tony was studying for his degree in public health, but now that he had one year to go in the program, he was making eyes at medical school—a financial impossibility of epic proportions seeing since he, like Sandy, was working for us in the flower shops.

Before the age of enlightenment, years ago, the families

Cacciamani and Roseman had despised one another. Romeo and I were raised from birth to scowl and spit when the other one's name was spoken. This was because our parents, rival Somerville florists, had loathed one another past the point of all reason, and this was because his mother and my father had briefly, secretly been in love with each other (isn't that always the way?), though no one else was privy to this information at the time.

After Romeo and I grew into adults who hated each other, our children fell in love, and we took it upon ourselves to squash their nascent happiness like a bug beneath our heel. It took us more than fifteen years and a couple of divorces before we all came together again, and this time Tony married Sandy and her two children, and I fell in love with his father.

It was a real happily-ever-after kind of thing, except that Tony and Sarah and the two kids couldn't afford a place of their own and were living with me, just as Romeo's other son, Alan, and his wife and their three kids were living with him. It wasn't that we didn't love them and weren't glad to help them, but still, wouldn't it be lovely to see a U-Haul backing down the driveway someday? I'd gone from fearing the empty-nest syndrome to fantasizing about it, without ever having the chance to experience it.

But there was no point in dwelling on the bigger picture

when there was a moment at hand to be seized. The house was empty except for the cat, who I had no qualms about scandalizing. I shrugged my coat to the floor. My purse hit with a thud. Romeo's coat exhaled in a pile of wool. Overcome by our unexpected good fortune, we started tugging at sweaters, pulling at shoes, kissing, kissing in the sheer happiness of two people who have forgotten about what we would be making for dinner or who would need homework help tonight.

In a gesture of romantic exuberance, Romeo put one arm around my back and looped the other under the backs of my knees and pulled me to his chest. The next thing I knew I was airborne, looking up into the front hallway's colonial brass light fixture, which I could now see needed some serious dusting. I let out a high laugh, so loud and girlish I did not recognize it as my own. "Put me down!"

"Someday," Romeo said, bouncing me up a half an inch to shift me in his arms.

I screamed, drunk with love, and slapped him madly on the back. "You're going to kill yourself. You're insane. Down! Down!"

He took three powerful and decisive steps toward the staircase, then, in a reckless moment that stunned us both, he started to climb the stairs.

"Romeo, don't!" It would have been so much more convincing had I been able to stop laughing from the giddy pleasure of it all. But when was the last time anyone had picked me up?

I can tell you, I was twenty-one, just back from my honeymoon and on the threshold of my new apartment. My then-husband Mort gallantly hoisted me over one shoulder like a feed sack, straightened up, said, "Oh, to hell with this," and set me down again, still on the wrong side of the door. Had he used just the slightest amount of momentum, he could have tossed me on the other side of the weather stripping, and I would have been in the living room. That was forty-two years and many pounds ago, and Mort, though tactless, was young and strong.

Before that, I was a little girl and my father was swinging me up toward the lights in his flower shop in a dizzying, carnation-scented moment of careless affection that he outgrew long before I was ready for him to put me down.

Other than that, my feet had been planted on terra firma where feet belonged, where feet needed to be right now. "Darling, really," I said to Romeo on the seventh stair of sixteen. "This is dangerous."

"I should carry you all the time," he said, a little bit of huff in his voice. "I should carry you into the store every morning."

His foot came down heavy on the ninth stair, and I felt him girding himself for the challenge of the tenth. I tightened my grasp around his neck and tried to inch myself up, to make myself lighter. I was nervous now. A little mistake had been made—a lovely gesture, a careless acceptance—but it had somehow gotten out of hand, and now I felt as if Romeo were trying to lug me up the side of Everest.

He wasn't going to put me down, and I knew it. We could both go straight backward, ass over teakettle to our inevitable deaths, but he wasn't going to give up midstaircase. For him that would be the same as calling me fat or calling himself weak, and neither of those two things was going to happen. So what if my daughter and his son and my two grandchildren came home to find Oompah-Loompah standing over the broken heap of our bodies, our clothes scattered lasciviously in all directions? We had lived in love and would die in love.

With enormous effort, we pushed on to the eleventh stair. I could feel the sledgehammer thump of his heart kicking against my ribs. "Almost there, my pet," he said, his voice weaker now.

We were both in our underwear, Romeo in the white briefs he favored (my ex-husband, my only prior exposure to men in their underwear, was a boxer man, and those briefs never failed to thrill me), and me in a mismatched satiny bra and cotton pants that I would not have chosen had I known where the day was headed when I got dressed.

It was not a comfortable arrangement. At this strange set of angles, an underwire from the left cup of my bra was about to pierce my sternum. Romeo's fingers, desperate for purchase, dug very, very deeply into my flesh, though I do not say this as a complaint.

Like his son Tony, Romeo was not a big man. He was not exactly short, but I was not exactly short myself. It had occurred to me on more than one occasion that our weights might be in the same ballpark. I didn't let myself think about it often, and I certainly never asked him, but I was thinking about it now. Romeo could be hefting twice his own body weight up my staircase, the kind of heroics reserved for tiny ants capable of carrying away an entire ruffled potato chip from a picnic blanket.

I did not have a single sexual thought in my head anymore. The ardor and lust that had swept me into his arms had vanished, and in their place was only the thought, *Please God, let us live. Let us make it to the top of the stairs.*

Thud, thud went his sock feet. *Thud, thud* went my heart. The thirteenth step. Unlucky thirteen. We were both silent as he pulled heroically toward the top. Romeo was gasping now, and I was taking in no air at all for fear that it might make me heavier. He went to kiss me but could only lay his damp cheek against my forehead. My rear end was slipping away from him, pulling down toward his knees, locked in a mortal bout with gravity.

"You're amazing," I said very quietly when he reached the top. "Now put me down."

"Almost there," he gasped, and again he gave me a little toss up to reposition the load, but this time I didn't toss at all. I was fixed in place, a leaden albatross nailed to his chest. I tried to pull myself higher as he trudged toward the bedroom, the very last one on the trail of tears down the hall.

We were so close. My bedroom was right there, just a few more feet. He made it through the door and into the soft autumnal light of a western exposure at sunset. I had to let him go all the way, then. If I jumped out of his arms this close to the bed it would have broken his heart, and so I stayed, my left hand clamped around my right wrist in a vise grip behind his neck. He took me to the edge and then, though I know he meant it to be a gentle settling, dropped me on the mattress.

I looked at him, still afraid to move. Was he gray? Was that grayness I was seeing? It was hard to tell. He straightened up a little, tentatively stretched down his arms to a position of straightness, and smiled.

"Are you okay?" I asked softly.

He nodded.

"That was very sweet. No one has ever done that before."

Not for me, not for anyone, not anywhere, except in the movies, which are made to fill our heads with silly romantic notions that would be impossible to live up to. They never tell you they use stand-ins: muscle men to carry; anorexic waifs to be carried; wheeling dollies wedged beneath their backsides to hoist them forward.

He leaned over and kissed me, and this time it was even sweeter. His kiss said: I would have a heart attack on a staircase for you. My kiss replied: I would gladly die with you in a tumbling crush of broken bones.

Love is passion and commitment, tenderness and endurance, but love is also memory. It is important to make a beautiful gesture from time to time, not only for the moment, but as something to hold on to in the future—so that when we were old, really old, I'd be able to hold his hand between our twin beds in the nursing home and think, *When you were merely sixty-three you carried me up a staircase.*

Romeo helped me with the hook on my bra because I have some arthritis in my thumbs that makes such things tricky for me. But then we were finally there, naked and together. Romeo crawled in beside me and I crawled on top of him and he screamed.

Chapter Two

TIME IS ELASTIC. EINSTEIN CAN GIVE YOU THE DE-
tails. I had always understood that in the moment of my death,
there would be time to reflect on the minutiae of human existence and my own contribution to it in a way that would be
both leisurely and profound. The two seconds before the car
crash stretches into hours. The rare surviving jumper from the
Golden Gate Bridge always tells the story of all the time he had
to work out his problems on the way down to the water. Ap-
parently they always come to the conclusion that life really was
a good thing after all.

What I hadn't known about this phenomenon is that it isn't
limited to your own death. The impending death of someone
you love as much as your own life can also do the trick. So
while it may seem insensitive that I would digress with Romeo's

last breath hanging in the balance, I would be remiss not to include the life that flashed before my eyes.

It was Sarah's. Maybe that's lucky: The kid was only eight so it didn't take a lot of time. In my split second of soul-crushing despair for having killed the only man I ever really loved, I saw my granddaughter: the freckles on her nose, which were her biological father's only contribution to her upbringing, her curly hair which, with a strong arm and a stiff brush, could be coaxed into honest-to-God ringlets that fell down her back like a Madame Alexander doll's. She was a sweet, affectionate kid with a good sense of humor, who had been a real pleasure until she fell into the vortex of the chocolate factory. I never thought it would have happened to her, though I guess that's what everyone says.

There was even a child in the film named Mike Teavee, who is one of the cautionary tales about the outcome of bad behavior. He is shrunken down to the height of a matchstick because he won't stop watching television. But Sarah pointed out that she watched no other television because she used her whole allotment of daily viewing to see Willie Wonka. Even then, she could only watch half of it a day because she was only allowed an hour on school nights (a schedule that was imposed out of *Wonka* desperation).

When I begged and reasoned and told her that she was a big girl now and it was time to give it up, the way she had given up sucking her thumb and carrying around that ratty little tailless bunny rabbit, she was resolute in her refusal. She said she couldn't give it up, she never would.

"It's *luck*," she said. "It's all about Charlie's luck and how important it is to keep believing in luck."

"So that's his luck," I said to her, "not yours."

"It is mine. When I watch it, it makes me lucky."

In this moment that popped up like a movie against my bedroom wall, Sarah was wearing a pink T-shirt with a pink heart smaller than a dime embroidered at the neckline. There was a smudge of something that looked sticky on her cheek. She is small for her age, and I always forget how powerful her reasoning can be.

"How does it make you lucky?"

"I watch it before I take a test, and I pass the test. I watch it before a game of kickball, and I get picked for the best team."

"But you also watch it before tests when you do lousy, and I've seen you come home from school when you didn't get picked for the best team—so it doesn't always work."

Sarah nodded patiently, sorry that I couldn't figure all of this out for myself. "That's when I watched without concentrating."

It occurred to me that maybe she had a little obsessive-compulsive disorder going on, and that instead of counting the number of steps it took to walk to the bus stop or having to tap the light switch ten times whenever she came into a room, she was watching Willie Wonka as a way of controlling her world. I should remember to talk to Sandy about this. "That's being superstitious, sweetheart. You're the one who gets the good grades. You get them when you try hard."

"It's more than that," she said darkly.

"Tell me, then."

"The movie keeps us safe. All of us."

"Safe from what? Fire? From getting sick?"

"From everything. Sometimes luck isn't a good thing that happens to you. Sometimes luck is everything staying just the way it is."

It surprised me that an eight-year-old could realize the implicit happiness in everyday life, but then, kids were a lot more sophisticated these days. "I agree with that, but again, it isn't the movie that does it."

She looked at me with her dark, searching eyes. "But what if you're wrong? Wouldn't it be better to keep watching, just to be sure?"

You don't really start making deals with God until the cards have turned against you, and in that split second of my eternity, I found myself wondering if I had disrupted the order of the universe by turning Sarah's movie off. What if she was right, and I had unwittingly thrown a rock in the smooth waters of our good fortune? I'm not saying I believe this, but the idea, with a hundred of its neighbors, came rushing past me.

But even if I had the chance to turn back the clock, I would still punch the TV's OFF button. I would always turn it off because it drove me insane. It drove Sandy insane, and it drove her husband Tony so insane, he would sit out on the back steps to study rather than stay inside with Willie Wonka, even when it meant having to shovel out a place for himself in the snow. It drove Little Tony insane, because sometimes he would be walking past the living room when it was on and he'd get stuck watching it. It caught him like a piece of flypaper, no matter how much he hated it, and once he could pull himself away he hated himself for watching, like a drunk hates himself after a bender.

In fact, the only person other than Sarah who could stand the movie at this point was my older daughter, Nora. If it was on when Nora came by, she would sit on the couch next to Sarah and stroke her hair and move her lips soundlessly to the words of the song. Nora, who had divided her days into perfectly scheduled ten-minute strips in her Palm Pilot, was never one for chitchat and hanging around—but somehow Gene

Wilder worked on her like a neural-inhibitor. I didn't understand it.

"It's like I told you," Sarah would explain to me. "She wants the luck."

Sarah's sense of luck was certainly becoming more specific. She had gone from believing that the movie was her general talisman for a safe and successful eight-year-old life, to thinking that the movie showed a clear way to profit. She had so completely entered into the world of Wonka that now she wanted her own golden ticket. Charlie Bucket got his from a candy bar. Sarah, understanding that such things did not exist in Somerville, had her sights set slightly higher. She decided to win the Massachusetts state lottery instead.

Oh, I suppose it started out innocently enough. One day, out of the blue, she asked if I would buy her a ticket when we were at the checkout line in the grocery store.

"A scratch ticket?"

She tilted up her chin and pursed her lips together, an interpretation of a child thinking that she had picked up from Shirley Temple movies. "No," she said slowly. "I think I want the Mega Millions."

The girl at the checkout, who had until this point been so thoroughly disengaged I would have thought she had been swallowed up by the pod people, sputtered out a little laugh.

She leveled her kohl-rimmed eyes at Sarah. "The other kids are angling for a Snickers," she said. "Or a Colt .45."

I gave her a chilly glance, but she had a point. When up against a can of malt liquor, a single lottery ticket didn't seem like much of a vice. "Do you want to pick your own numbers?" I asked.

"May I?" Sarah said brightly, still in Temple-mode, which accounted for the correct grammar. I pulled out a dollar bill and handed it over. There was no dithering over the numbers. Sarah knew exactly what she wanted.

The kid was canny, I had to give her that. She'd hit up one adult and then another, always remembering to space us out so as to never look suspicious. She asked casually, as if it were the last thing in the world she really wanted but it had just crossed her mind. She never asked for more than a dollar at a time. Over and over again, we fell for it. Her secret plan was to win big. She wanted the entire chocolate factory.

So, that was my elastic time moment, naked, looking down at Romeo. I thought about having luck, and the insatiable human greed of wanting more of it. And all of that happened in a split second though it seemed like half an hour. He was still screaming.

I scrambled over him to the other side of the bed and grabbed the phone. I don't know what people did before telephones.

Even if you couldn't save a life, at least you had a sense of purpose in the crisis now. "Hang on," I said. "I'm calling an ambulance."

"Don't." Romeo's eyes were pressed closed tightly, and his neck was slightly arched, as if he was trying to push the crown of his head into his pillow. I remembered the position from a yoga class I took years ago. It was called the Fish. He was sweating like crazy.

"What do you mean, don't?" I was in full panic mode now. "You're having a heart attack!" I should have taken that CPR class they'd offered at the Y. Was it five breaths and ten pumps, or the other way around?

"No—heart—attack." The words seemed to be harder for him than carrying me up the stairs. His teeth were locked together.

"Listen to me," I said in a loud voice, as if the problem were his hearing. "Even if this isn't a heart attack, it's clearly an ambulance worthy situation."

Romeo still hadn't opened his eyes, and the edges of his lips looked slightly blue. "Call—Al."

I stood there for a second, blinking, then I sank down next to Romeo and touched his hand. My heart fell five flights of stairs. "Father Al? You want me to call your priest?"

I saw the slightest movement of his head and then he yelped and cringed. It was a nod.

I started to cry. I put my head in my hands.

"Now," Romeo reminded me. His breathing was very shallow.

I went to the bedside table for a phone book. Wouldn't it be something to want to turn to God with your last breath? I guess I'd want to see my daughters, assuming that Romeo was already with me. Maybe I'd want to see my grandchildren or my best friend, Gloria. I couldn't imagine that religion would even occur to me in that moment, as it hadn't occurred to me since Sandy had her Bat Mitzah the year she turned thirteen.

But as I put my hands on the phone book, I knew with utter clarity who I would want to see in my final moments on earth: I'd want to see the admitting doctor at Mass General Hospital. If I were going to die, then the last person leaning over me better be someone who was doing everything in his power to keep it from happening. I shut the phone book with a decisive thump. "This is insane. You're going to the hospital."

"It's 8-2-4-7-7-8-9," Romeo said, though every digit extracted a toll on him.

I dialed.

"Julie!" Father Al said when he picked up after the second ring. "You've made my day."

"You knew it was me?" I said. The Catholics were always surprising me.

"Caller ID," he said.

I wasn't sure it was right for a priest to have caller ID. Who was he avoiding? "Romeo's here, and he's very sick. He said I couldn't call an ambulance. He said I had to call you." I started crying again and had a hard time saying the last sentence. "Al, I think he might be dying."

"Not," Romeo managed to get out.

"He says he's not dying," I told Al. I picked up the corner of the bedspread and wiped my eyes. "But I don't believe him."

"Ask him if it's his back," Al said.

"Is it your back?"

"Yes," Romeo said. The word was somewhat calmer than the others. I didn't think the pain was lessening, but he seemed to be making peace with it.

"Poor Romeo," Al sighed. "The last time it was horrible. It was biblical, really. But he's right about not wanting the ambulance. When it happened before, they ruptured a disc on top of everything else when they were getting him on the stretcher. Is he upstairs or downstairs?"

"Upstairs," I said, feeling guilty.

This sealed the deal for Al. "He's better off if you just let him lie still. I'll come over with Dominic; he's right here with me now. I'm sure that's why he's having you call. Ask him if he wants to see Dominic."

"Dominic?" I said to Romeo.

Something crossed his face that was almost like peace. "Dominic," he said.

After Al had assured me that Romeo wasn't going to die, and promised that they would make record time getting to my house, I hung up the phone. "You're going to be okay," I said to Romeo. "They're on their way."

"Yes," he said softly. He looked like he had been shot. He looked like he needed a bottle of whiskey and a knife to bite on.

"Is there anything I can get for you? A heating pad? Some coffee?"

"No." I saw him take a running jump at the words *thank you,* but he gave up after passing the "th" sound.

"I won't ask you anything else. I'm just going to sit here and you don't have to say another word." I kept two fingers lightly on the top of his hand and thought about how much I loved him, how lucky we had been to find each other just at the moment when other people were giving up on love altogether.

The light from the windows was almost gone, though it wasn't even five o'clock. I switched on the lamp beside the bed so I could watch his breathing, which seemed impossibly shallow and irregular. I was crying a little again, part from love and part from his pain and mostly from my stupidity at letting him carry me up the stairs.

"Talk." Romeo opened one eye a little and tried to smile at me.

I took a deep breath and did my best to find a steady voice. Romeo liked to hear me talk, he was always telling me the sound of my voice made him feel better.

"I'm worried about you. I know that's not what you want to hear. I love you." Talking was a funny thing. I could think of a million things to say until someone asked me what they were; and then they flew out of my head like hummingbirds.

"Do you ever think about luck, about the way things turn out? What if your parents had stayed in Italy? Or what if my grandparents had gone to New York? They did for awhile, you know. They had cousins in Brooklyn, and they stayed there for months after the boat ride over here, but my mother kept saying it was too dirty, and she wanted to move again. Your parents could have sold fish and mine could have made hats and they never would have met and hated each other and we never would have met and fallen in love."

In my mind I saw myself passing Romeo on the street, strangers to one another. I'm sure it happened all the time, true love missed by circumstance. "It's like every second is a chance, a choice between turning right or left, and when you stack those millions of choices on top of each other, what are the chances that we'd get here?"

Romeo took a deeper breath, and I thought I saw something in his neck relax a little. It made me feel hopeful, and the hope kept me talking.

"What if our parents had both made chocolates? It sounds like a good idea. When I was a kid I would have been in heaven. There was a girl in my fifth-grade class, Nancy Tilsman, her father owned Tilsman's Drugs. She got to have any candy bar she wanted after school every day. She could go to the rack and take anything that struck her fancy and not even ask. She told me once that she basically owned all the candy anyway, because it was all her father's and what was his was practically hers. I remember thinking at the time that there could be no luck on earth greater than that.

"But now I think I never would have lasted in the chocolate business. I would have gotten fat, my skin would have broken out, and I would have cashed out the first year I was in charge. But I'm always glad to see the flowers. No matter what's going on in my life, the flowers always make me happy. Even when things were at their very worst, when Mort left me and I just about bankrupted the store, and I had to work around the clock just to hold on to things, I never once resented the flowers.

"The way I see it, we have a lot to be grateful for. We have each other and we have our families and we have the flowers, and up until about twenty minutes ago we had our health. I have to say we're doing pretty well."

I don't know who I was trying to convince, me or him, but the inspirational lecture seemed to make both of us feel better. Romeo lifted his fingers and I slid mine underneath them, and he lightly pressed down. It was a moment, pure and unsustainable.

Then I heard the back door open, and Tony and Sarah started shouting out for Grandma.

Chapter Three

I WAS NAKED, BUT STILL HAD THE PRESENCE OF mind not to move too quickly so I didn't bounce poor Romeo. I stood up carefully and made a quick dash to the closet for my bathrobe, a shameful abomination of ten-year-old chenille that looked like the primary function of its long, hard life had been to wax floors.

"One second," I called. I covered up my beloved, who was mostly under the covers anyway. "I'm going to go put out the fire," I said to him. "Don't go anywhere."

"Hah," he said weakly.

I was three steps down the staircase of our recent undoing when Little Tony and Sarah and Sandy rounded the corner into the entry hall from the kitchen. All of our eyes landed on the same pile of clothing locked together in a loving embrace on the floor.

"You didn't hang your coats in the closet," Sarah said in a self-satisfied voice. I was always reminding her to do just that. Fortunately, she didn't see it was more than coats on the floor.

The way I saw it, I had two options: I could ignore the clothes, or I could pick them up very fast. I decided to pretend I didn't see them.

"Are you sick?" Tony said.

"No, honey, I'm not sick, but—"

"You're in your bathrobe."

"I am, that's right."

"And you've been crying," Sarah said.

I touched my hand to my face, and my eyes were still wet. I had been crying over the very thought that something could happen to Romeo, and when I remembered that, my eyes welled up again.

Sandy was looking at the clothes and looking at me and doing the math in her head. She stared at my bare feet and ankles, and chances are she was making a correct assumption that the bareness went all the way up. "Why don't you kids go do your homework," she said in a flat voice.

"I want to show Grandma my new shoes," Sarah said.

"I'll look at them in just one minute, sweetheart. Sandy, can I talk to you for a second?"

She looked at me sternly, the way I had looked at her when I caught her sneaking in the back door in the middle of the night from a date with Tony Cacciamani, when she was a junior in high school. She took several exaggerated steps through the piles of clothing (she *could* have walked around them) and I was heading down the stairs as the doorbell rang.

"I'll get the door!" Tony said.

"I want to get the door!" his sister said.

"I said I was going to get it first!"

Was it possible that Al could get here so fast?

"You always get to get the door. Mom, he always gets to get the door!"

Sandy, who was only two feet from the door, just leaned over and opened it.

In all of my confusion I had never thought to ask Al who Dominic was, but when they stepped inside the entry hall, it was plain to see that Dominic was Al's younger brother. They both had the same heavy salt-and-pepper hair, the same broad shoulders and beefy arms that made them look like they should be unloading crates onto docks. Al had on his regular uniform, black pants and a black shirt and a black cotton zip-up jacket, while Dominic wore khakis and a brown leather aviator's jacket.

"Hi Al," Sandy said, and the children ran over and threw

their arms around him, calling, "Father Al! Father Al." They loved Al, and more than that, it cracked them up to say his name. They never got over the delicious strangeness of addressing someone who wasn't their father as Father. They could not say it enough. I thought briefly of my mother stirring in her grave to see her progeny embracing a Catholic priest, but the truth is, I would have hugged Al myself were I not feeling so naked beneath my robe.

"I thought Romeo was the one who was sick," he said. There was no reference to funny business in his tone; Al was remarkably without guile.

"I thought she was sick, too," Tony said, excited by the coincidence of jumping to the same conclusion.

"Romeo's sick?" Sandy asked.

"He's hurt his back," I said.

Sandy lowered her eyebrows slightly. "Where is he?"

"Upstairs." I tried very hard to banish any note of sheepishness from my voice, but I wasn't very successful. We were all more or less standing in a pool of our clothing. I had made a poor choice earlier when I decided to let them lie.

"Romeo! Romeo! Romeo!" Sarah called and bounded past me up the stairs. She took them two at a time, and in a flash she was on the second floor, a gazelle clearing a hillock in a single, graceful leap.

"Sarah!" Sandy barked just as the girl was reaching for the bedroom door. Everyone froze. It was a dazzling trick that Sandy could pull off when absolutely necessary. Wisely, she did not overuse it. The Bark was reserved for only the most dire of occasions.

"I was just . . ." Sarah began.

"Downstairs!" Sandy said.

Sarah considered putting up an argument, but then thought better of it. She began to slink down, one wrist trailing limply over the banister.

Al cleared his throat nervously. Sandy had always looked so unassuming, and now he would have to rethink her completely. "This is my brother, Dominic."

Poor Dominic. He must have thought we were a flock of loons. "Welcome to the fun house," I said, and shook his hand.

"Pleasure," he said.

"Dominic's a doctor," Al said. "You probably know that already."

"Our mother used to say that having a priest and a doctor in the family meant everybody was covered one way or the other." Dominic held up a plastic shopping bag from CVS. "I brought a few things by." It wasn't exactly a black alligator bag but I'd take it.

"I really appreciate you making a house call," I said, holding the neck of my bathrobe closed with one hand. "Especially on such short notice. I didn't think you'd get here so quickly."

"We just finished Mass," Al said. "Saturday night is a good time to call. You got me on the cell."

"Priests have cell phones now?" I asked. I don't know why this surprised me. I wouldn't have been surprised to see a rabbi with a cell phone, at least a reform rabbi, but priests still seemed to have one foot in the middle ages, what with the incense and all.

"Did you say Romeo is sick?" Sandy said. Sandy was like one of those very clever black-and-white dogs that can teach a sheep to ride a bicycle. She was trying to cut the flock in half, herd the adults upstairs and the children into the kitchen. I had a suspicion she wanted to pick up the clothing.

"He's this way," I said, and started walking up.

"I've never seen the upstairs of your house," Father Al said brightly.

"Romeo?" I said quietly as I opened the door and brought our company into my bedroom.

The clothes on the floor of the entry hall looked bad—a shirt, a sweater, two pairs of pants, all those shoes touching laces—but maybe that could be written off to very poor housekeeping. In the bedroom, however, the underwear told a different story. The underwear was intermingling on the floor. In one deft move, I kicked it under the bed.

Romeo looked like he had frozen into the last moment I had seen him. Every muscle in his face, the way he held his arms, everything about him was exactly the same.

"Oh, Romeo," Father Al said, and shook his head at the sight of so much pain.

Dominic, on the other hand, didn't seem to be bothered at all. "Didn't see you at Mass last week, buddy," he said. "Your mother must be lightening up on you."

Romeo's eyes opened into slits. He made a sound that was clearly intended to be "hah" but it didn't quite come out as "hah." It sounded more like a sharp exhale.

"Horsing around with a back like yours." Dominic shook his head and starting rummaging through his bag of tricks. "We're not kids anymore, Romeo."

"You shouldn't give him a lecture when he can't even talk back to you," Al said.

Romeo gave a small smile.

"You think he can't talk back to me now, just you wait." Dominic tore open a little foil packet and pulled back the sheets enough to rub an alcohol swab over a small spot on Romeo's hip. Then he fixed up a shot. "You know the expression, 'You made your bed, and now you're going to have to lie in it?' Well, that's the story. You stay exactly where you are. The only other place you're going to be going is to the hospital for surgery."

"He's going to need surgery?" I asked.

"Maybe not, if he can stay still and let himself get better." He slid the needle into Romeo's hip, and I winced, though Romeo never seemed to notice.

"What is that?"

"Demerol and Phenergan. It will knock him out and keep him from throwing up. It's a terrible thing to throw up when you've broken your back."

"I *broke* his back?"

Both Al and Dominic turned to look at me, and Romeo used his last word to whisper, kindly, "No."

"We won't know for sure without an X-ray, but chances are he has a compression fracture. Just think of it as two of his vertebrae moving a little closer together. At least that's what he had ten years ago, and when you have one, it stands to reason you're going to have two. But it's nobody's fault." Dominic stopped and reconsidered this. "Well, it's his fault. Whatever he was doing, it's pretty safe to say he shouldn't have been doing it."

I was so distraught, I wondered if there was anything left in that vial for me. Then we could be laid out side by side, Romeo and Julie, the star-crossed aging lovers who fell prey to their own passions.

"How long does he have to stay in bed?"

"It could be a week, it could be considerably more. It depends on how he heals up. Even when he's up, he's going to mostly be down. You have to keep him in bed."

"I'll try my best." Standing there naked in my tatty bathrobe, the comment felt tawdry.

Dominic patted me on the shoulder. He could have made any number of jokes and had a nice laugh at my expense or Romeo's, but he took the high road and gave me a pleasant smile. "I'll swing by in the morning to check on him. You take good care of him. If you need something, you call me. We go all the way back. We always felt sorry for Romeo being an only child—we used to let him tag along."

"There were thirteen of us," Al said.

Dominic capped the spent syringe and dropped it back into the bag, then he scrawled out a series of prescriptions. "These are for pain, and he's going to need them. Whatever he needs, I'll be here."

"And I'll be here, too," Al said.

"If he decides to opt for faith healing over Demerol," his brother said. "But I think he should stick with the drugs. This man you are in love with has a very bad back." I thought I detected a certain amount of pity in his voice, like I had been the unwitting recipient of damaged goods that I was now stuck with.

Al and Dominic offered to show themselves out, and I stood by the bed, watching the man I loved melt into a deep puddle of drug-induced sleep. Kink by kink, he let go of his waking life and spread across the sheets. I could tell just by looking at him that he wasn't going to be coming around anytime soon.

I sat down very carefully on the bed beside him and held his hand. For that minute I could see him as a boy of six or seven, worn out and hard asleep after a day of summer baseball. I could see him as a father at thirty, up all night with croupy babies and completely exhausted, or a businessman of fifty, falling asleep on his flower-arranging table after a giant wedding.

My dear Romeo. So he had a bad back he hadn't mentioned before. Believe me, there were things going wrong with my own machinery that I hadn't been so quick to share. Well, I wouldn't let him carry the boxes of flowers in from the truck anymore. Everything would be fine.

There was a light tap on the door, and Sandy stuck her head inside, her curls conveying a sense of franticness. "Is he okay? Al said his back was a mess."

"He'll be fine," I said, resting assured in my own sudden sense of peace.

Sandy slipped inside the door, our clothes neatly folded in her arms, the shoes balanced on top. "I brought you these." She put them on top of the dresser.

"Thank you. I'm sorry I didn't get things picked up."

"I was going to give you a hard time, you know, before I realized that Romeo was hurt." She sat down on the little straight-backed chair beside my desk and looked at the two of us. "The truth is, I wish Tony and I could be alone in the house every now and then. Privacy is hard to come by around here."

"Maybe we should have a sign-up sheet." Sandy and I really were in the same boat. She was married to the son and I was in love with the father and with all of us in the house together with two kids, it was just about impossible to find five minutes alone.

From downstairs I heard Little Tony wail, then I heard the Candyman start to sing again. Sandy sighed and shook her head. "There she goes."

"She's going to do us all in," I said. "You know that."

"Mom!" Tony cried from outside the door.

Sandy sighed again and pushed up out of her chair heavily, like a foreman going to deliver a guilty verdict. She opened the door halfway and touched her son's head gently. "I know."

"I can't stand it!"

"Listen, go in your room and put your Walkman on. It's all you can do. I need to spend some time with Grandma right now."

Tony peered around his mother to where I sat on the bed with my sleeping Romeo. "Is he okay?"

Tony was a sweet boy, maybe too sensitive for his own good, but genuinely loving and concerned for others.

"Sure he's okay," I said. "He just needs to get some sleep. Go tell Sarah to turn the volume down. Tell her that Romeo is trying to rest."

Tony smiled hugely. So rarely did we give him the opportunity to exercise any real authority over his little sister. As he ran down the stairs, he screamed out her name.

"Sarah! Grandma said—"

Sandy shut the door. "She's become so fixated on this whole lottery thing."

"It's 234 million dollars," I said. "Most residents of Massachusetts, Vermont, and New Hampshire are fixated on it."

"I'm worried about what's going to happen to her when she doesn't win. What if she grows up to be a compulsive gambler?"

"From what I understand, compulsive gamblers are people who win at first, then spend the rest of their lives trying to re-create the experience. Sarah's never won a dime."

"I still think we should cut her off. The lottery isn't meant for eight-year-olds."

"So we'll stop buying her tickets."

Sandy wrapped a curl around her finger and pulled it down until it was straight. "Can you imagine it though, if she did win? We could move out of here and buy a house. Big Tony could go to medical school. Both Tonys could go to medical school if they wanted to. We could *buy* a medical school."

"Sandy," I said in a low voice.

She dropped her face to her hands. "I'm sorry. I'm falling prey to Wonka-thought. It's hard not to, sometimes. It's like living in an Orwell novel; you hear the same propaganda day after day and after awhile it's hard not to believe it."

"Satisfying and delicious," I said wearily. I picked up sleeping Romeo's hand and petted it. "He doesn't even hear us."

When I was a little girl I was always losing my parents, or they were losing me. They would take me to market before the sun came up to buy flowers, and I would get interested in a stray cat or a straight line of ladybugs walking over the face of a Gerber daisy, and when I looked up they would be gone. "Just stay where you are," my father would always say. "If you stay put, then we'll know where to find you."

That seemed to be the advice that stuck with me for the rest of my life. I stayed put in Somerville, stayed put in the house Mort and I bought together with my parents' help when I was pregnant with Nora, stayed put in the family business long after my parents had died and Mort had left. Now I was staying put in my own bed next to Romeo, and one by one everyone was finding me.

Big Tony sailed up the stairs and through the door without so much as a tap. The Cacciamanis were not inclined toward knocking.

"Dad!"

Big Tony wore a close-trimmed beard and a pair of green carpenter's pants with various loops hanging off the side in case he felt like carrying hammers. He was boyishly handsome and boyish in his heartfelt intensity. He *loved* Sandy, he *loved* her kids, he *loved* public health. I even believed he had come to love me, and oh, did he love his father. He picked up Romeo's hand and immediately dropped his fingers down to feel his pulse.

"Why isn't he waking up? Why isn't he in the hospital?"

Sandy came over to her husband and wrapped her arms around his waist. "It's his back. Dominic said he was going to be fine."

"He gave him a shot to help him relax," I said, scooting off the bed to give him some room. I had to get dressed. I could not put this off another minute.

"He has an awful back," Tony said. An awful back, one step beyond a bad back. "What was he doing?"

"Tony," Sandy said, in a kind voice.

Not only did I have to get dressed, I had to figure out a way to get some clothes on Romeo before the neighbors started dropping by to pay their respects.

"Dominic said he thought Romeo would do better if he just stayed where he was for now."

"The last time they tried to move him it was a disaster." Tony put his father's hand down gently on top of the covers. "Poor Dad."

Sandy looked at me, then at her husband. "He's going to be fine. I know he's hurt, but it's just his back."

Tony shrugged. "Maybe it'll be different this time."

"So how was it last time?"

"He was in bed for two months. He nearly went out of his mind. My mother, God rest her soul, she nearly went out of her mind."

I pulled the belt of my bathrobe tighter, a clear sign that I was ready to face whatever lay ahead. "We'll get through this," I said.

"Sure we will. I'll call the flower shops and let them know

you won't be coming back in to close," Tony said wistfully, and gave Sandy a little sideways hug. Then he looked up at me. "By the way, Nora's downstairs. She wanted me to tell you. She was on her way up but she got stuck watching that wretched movie with Sarah."

Chapter Four

A FEW WORDS ABOUT NORA, MY OLDEST DAUGH-
ter: She has a way of looking at me that makes me feel like
I've just picked up a sterling silver picture frame off an end
table of a fancy hotel and stuck it in my pocket; her expression
toward me is one of perpetual incredulity, shame, and weary
disappointment. I was well acquainted with this look, having
worn it for the first nineteen years of Nora's life. The difference
was she usually *had* palmed a frame, and I was timid about removing a single peppermint from the large bowl of free candy
at our local Italian restaurant. Nora, so reckless in her youth, so
careless, so mean, rounded a huge hairpin curve in her early
twenties and became the doyenne of overachievement. I would
not be incorrect in saying she swipes an iron over her gym
socks. She made a blistering load of money selling real estate,
and her husband, Alex, brought in an equal haul doing tax law.

They were bright and disciplined and highly scheduled. There was an agenda for everything they did, and children were never on the agenda.

But then they were. In the last year Nora started showing up at my house more and more, bringing over presents for Little Tony and Sarah, being the fun aunt who took them for pizza on a school night. One day last spring out of the blue, she said that she wanted to come with me to take Tony to one of his first baseball games of the season, then she sat in the bleachers under a big hat and cried.

"What is it?" I asked her.

Nora slipped her fingers beneath her Jackie-O sunglasses and wiped carefully under her eyes. "I want to have a baby."

I looked around us. There were no babies in the stands; where had this come from? "Since when?" I whispered. I was afraid someone would overhear us and laugh us out of the park. Anyone who had ever spent five minutes around Nora knew she most certainly did not want a baby. I had asked her about it once, not long after she and Alex were married. I remember her answer quite specifically. "Babies are for losers," she'd said.

"I've always wanted a baby," she said.

Nora was not a crier. Sandy would sob at the mere mention of a Kodak commercial, but Nora did not cry. Therefore, seeing her cry made me extremely nervous.

"No, you didn't."

She just kept looking at the tough green grass, the field of little boys in dirty uniforms who dreamed of being Red Sox. "Of course I did, but Alex was in law school, then I was buying out the real-estate firm, and we were both so busy. There was never time."

"You *never* wanted a baby. Nora, you've always hated babies. You hate children. You wouldn't even speak to Sandy when she got pregnant."

"I was jealous. No one ever thought about how hard that was for me."

"Does this have to do with your father?" I had to ask. Mort now had three children: Nora, age forty; Sandy, age thirty-six; and Nicolette, age not quite two. My sixty-five-year-old ex-husband was out in Seattle toting around a toddler with his fortysomething-year-old wife. There he was, finally picking up his Social Security check, and he was back to diapers and spit-up and booster shots. A child at his age seemed less like procreation and more like straight-out punishment. I saw it as God's retribution on Mort for running off with Lila in the first place.

"What do you think—Dad and Lila have a baby, and so now I want one, too?"

"I guess not. If anything, your father makes a convincing case for birth control."

Tony got his turn up at bat, and after two mad swings into the air he managed to pop off a small bunt and we stood up and cheered.

Nora had to raise her voice to be heard over the roar of the crowd. "Alex and I have started in vitro fertilization."

The pitcher grabbed the ball that had rolled toward him and threw it to the first baseman, where it arrived long before Tony. There was a brief collective moan, and we all sat down again.

How had we gotten to in vitro already? Nora had always liked high tech. She was the first person I knew to get a plasma screen TV. She was all about doing things in whatever way was considered state of the art. It seemed possible that she had skipped the natural middle part of this process and shot straight to the end.

"Did you try . . ." I was unable to finish the sentence.

Nora pulled her sunglasses down on her nose and peered at me over the top. "Of course we tried. We've been trying for a long time."

"Well, you never said anything."

"I never said that Alex and I had sex? Forgive me for not

mentioning that. Yes, Mother, Alex and I have sex." She pushed her sunglasses back. "We just can't get pregnant."

"I'm sorry." I was trying quickly to shift everything I knew about my daughter. This was Nora, who referred to baby showers as ritualized extortion. Nora, who asked to be moved in restaurants and on airplanes if a sleeping baby was located within five tables or ten rows. Nora of the personal trainer and the immaculate Lexus. Nora wanted to have a baby.

"I'm only forty," she said. "Everybody waits until forty now. Forty is the new thirty."

I wondered if anyone had let her ovaries in on this piece of news.

"When I was forty you were a junior in high school," I said without a trace of malice. "I sat up nights with the phone in my lap waiting for the police to call while you rode around town on the back of some boy's motorcycle. Do you really want to be waiting for that call when you're fifty-seven?"

"My children won't ever do that to me. They'll be very responsible. They'll be like Alex."

And then, thank heavens, she laughed.

Nora bought Little Tony baseball cards and Crosby, Stills, Nash, and Young CDs, which seemed to speak to him deeply. For Sarah she bought lottery tickets. Often she went to the trouble of unwrapping a Hershey bar and putting the tickets next to the chocolate, then rewrapping the whole thing.

Sarah and Nora sat together in front of the television set on Wednesday nights and waited for the lottery drawing. Sarah explained to Nora the principles of luck and how it would be better if she could come early so that they could watch *Willie Wonka and the Chocolate Factory* before the Mega Million picks. Sarah also sent Nora into the kitchen to intercede on her behalf with Sandy so that they could watch the whole thing through in one sitting (much luckier.)

One day, Sandy told Nora, "I have a rule about television."

Nora gave a quick roll of her eyes. "You have a rule about everything."

"That's right," Sandy said. "I do. I have a rule about lottery tickets, too. You have to stop buying her so many."

"You buy them for her."

"I buy her one a week, and I shouldn't even do that. You come in here with ten at a time."

I was sitting at the kitchen table, pretending to read the paper. I did not admit at this moment that I bought Sarah a ticket and usually two most weeks, and I had certainly seen her tap Romeo to pick one up for her when she was at one of the flower shops. Was she getting other tickets from other adults?

Was she standing in the parking lot of the Stop & Shop after school, asking strangers to take her allowance to buy her a lottery ticket?

From the living room I could hear the opening theme music, that syrupy confection that portended all the candy that was to come. "Aunt Nooorraaaa!" Sarah sang. "It's on!"

"I'll be right there," Nora called. "Look," she said to Sandy. "I'm going to watch that movie. If Sarah is in there, that's up to her."

Sandy was an adult, a wife and a mother of two, but she was still afraid of her older sister. "It's a good thing you never had children," she said in defeat. She hadn't meant it as a blow; she had no idea that Nora wanted one.

All summer long and through the fall, I would find Nora in the living room with Sarah sprawled across her lap. Often they silently mouthed the words to the songs. Nora had completely destroyed any rules Sandy had about watching the movie too often. If Sandy complained, Nora would simply pop the tape out of the VCR and take both it and Sarah back to her house.

Often Nora's presence in the living room would take me by surprise. I would simply be walking through my house, and there she would be. I was starting to wonder if she was having problems with Alex, if soon both of my daughters would be living at home again.

"When did you get here?" I asked, one day.

"Half an hour ago." She didn't take her eyes off the screen.

"Can you stay for dinner?"

Nora gave one slight turn of her head to indicate no, she would be dining at home this evening. She looked glazed over, exhausted, while the fat orange Oompah-Loompahs danced in front of her and the real Oompah-Loompah lay across her loafers like a tiny beached whale. Her pants were not exactly wrinkled, but they did not have a sharp crease, and she was wearing one of Alex's dress shirts with the sleeves rolled up. It was a very un-Nora look. Sarah was wearing Nora's favorite Hermès scarf tied around her head and neck like Grace Kelly in *To Catch a Thief.*

"Nora, get up and come into the kitchen. I have to talk to you," I said.

"In a minute," she said.

In A Minute. That was the only thing she ever said to me when she was a teenager. Where was Alex? Why wasn't she working? Nora never had any time for anyone or anything, yet now she seemed to be taking up permanent residence in my living room.

I picked up the clicker and shut the television off. Sarah immediately snapped up and started howling like I had stepped on her head. "Nora. In the kitchen. Right now."

Nora looked up at me and blinked. She didn't seem to notice the fact that Sarah was screaming. She dislodged the cat and pushed herself off the couch to follow me sullenly into the kitchen. As I left the room I turned the television back on and Sarah breathed a deep sigh of relief. The Oompah-Loompahs took up exactly where they had left off, and the cat collapsed back on the floor.

"What?" she said to me. She had that same hollowed-out expression she used to wear as a teenager, and for a minute I thought of asking her if she was smoking pot again.

"What? Nora, you're lying on the couch watching *Willie Wonka* for the fiftieth time. Your best friend is your eight-year-old niece. You don't seem to be spending much time at home anymore. Don't you think something's wrong?"

"Nothing's wrong," she said heavily, and turned back to follow the music into the living room.

"This conversation isn't over."

Nora looked at me with a squint. "Why, because you need more information about my personal life? I'm tired, okay? Is that what you want to hear? I'm tired of Alex giving me shots every night and tired of hoping I won't get my period, and I'm tired of feeling like a failure. I'm used to being very good at whatever I put my mind to, and I have to tell you, my mind is on having a baby and I'm getting nowhere. As for spending time with Sarah, I like it. She believes that good things are going to happen, and that's good for me. There was a woman in my doctor's office today who was forty-nine years old and she got pregnant, bang! And I just sat there, and said, 'Oh, that's so nice for you.'"

"Who would want to have a baby at forty-nine?" I genuinely could not imagine it. I remembered a woman who had a daughter in Girl Scouts with Sandy and two more daughters at home. She turned up pregnant at forty-five, and she cried about it for three weeks.

"Lots of people!" Nora said. "You just don't understand. You wanted a baby, and so you had a baby. It wasn't any problem for you at all."

"I was twenty-three when I had you. I would have gotten pregnant if I'd bumped against the washing machine."

"So you think it's my own fault for waiting?" Nora did not say this in an angry way. She was asking me. She had clearly given the subject of fault and blame a great deal of consideration.

"Of course I don't think it's your fault. But Nora, you have a very happy life. You love your work, you love Alex. You have a million things going for you, and all of those things are going to be there if you don't have a baby."

"Hurry up!" Sarah yelled. "It's almost time."

It was time for the lovely Dawn Hayes to call the lottery numbers as they popped out of the machine. Nora turned away and walked into the living room, and I followed her. Sandy wandered in with Little Tony and even Big Tony, who usually made a real point of staying away from the television set, came to watch.

Sarah had a piece of paper and a pencil ready, and she wrote the numbers down when each white Ping-Pong ball shot up through the tube and Dawn read them out. Everything about her face was focused. She was channeling the spirit of Charlie Bucket, the poor but hopeful hero of Mr. Wonka's chocolate factory. She had every intention of winning.

"Thirty-seven, nineteen, seven . . ." Sarah repeated each number out loud.

It wasn't a match. She knew her tickets by heart, and even though she would go upstairs and pull out the envelope where she kept them—in her left bedroom slipper in the far right-hand corner of her closet—to double-check just in case, she wasn't a winner. No golden ticket.

"The odds are millions and millions to one," Sandy said, and reached down to pet Sarah's hair.

"It just means there'll be more money next week," Sarah said bravely. "It'll be even better to win then."

"That's assuming that nobody won this week," Little Tony said. "In which case the whole thing goes back to zero."

Sarah looked truly shocked that even an older brother could say such a cruel thing. "I'm going to win."

Nora picked up the child's hand and kissed it. "Of course you are."

But that was all several weeks and many drawings ago. By the time Romeo had crunched down the tiny vertebrae in his back, it was almost Halloween and neither Sarah nor Nora had won their separate lotteries, though they went to the television as religiously as Father Al went to church, to try and bend God's favor in their direction.

✎

I finally, gratefully, managed to jump into a pair of sweatpants and a big flannel shirt and came down the stairs in my sneakers. I made a vow to stay in my clothes forever, just to be on the safe side. Nora was back on the couch with one arm tossed around Sarah's shoulder, and they were watching the movie—or Sarah was watching the movie and Nora was gazing fondly at the top of Sarah's head.

"How's Romeo?" Nora whispered when I came into the room.

"Not so good. He'll be fine eventually, but right now, not great."

"I'm sorry," Nora said, but frankly, she didn't look so sorry. She looked like she was about to start laughing hysterically.

"Are you okay?" I said.

"She's pregnant," Sarah said, never once taking her eyes off the television where Veruca Salt, the rich little girl who was the worst one of them all, demanded that the workers in her father's factory unwrap the candy bars faster. "And I'm going to win the lottery." Sarah held up a dozen shiny new lottery tickets.

Nora rapped Sarah lightly on the top of the head. "It's my news. I should have been the one to tell."

"You weren't fast enough," Sarah said. "Anyway, you just said you were going to tell her. I never told her before today."

"Sarah knew?" Was it possible that I felt jealous of my eight-year-old granddaughter?

"I guessed," Sarah said.

"Oh, Nora," I leaned down to wrap this woman in my arms who was my first baby, my own pink-cheeked girl. I'll admit it, I didn't think it was such a great idea for Nora and Alex to pursue a pregnancy at this point, but the second it was a reality, every lingering doubt I had flew out of my head, and I was only completely happy. "When are you due?"

"Early April. I just came from the doctors', and he said things looked very strong. That was how he put it, 'strong.'"

I ran the numbers quickly in my head. "You're four months pregnant?"

"Three and a half."

I looked at her. It was true. I hadn't noticed it before, but there was something going on underneath her loose-fitting shirt. Still, I couldn't believe that she'd been sitting on my couch all this time wearing a long face when she already knew the truth. Nora was never a big one for sharing, but this seemed impossible. "You've been pregnant all this time, and you never told me?"

"I didn't want to get anybody's hopes up until things looked good. Even now." She shrugged in a peculiar attempt to seem casual about things. "You never know."

"But everything's going to be fine." Technically speaking I didn't know this, but as her mother I felt certain.

"It didn't work the last time," Nora said.

"Last time?"

"She had two miscarriages before," Sarah said.

This broke my heart a thousand times over.

"Miscarriage might be too strong a word. It was only after a few weeks." Nora stretched out her hands and inspected her cuticles, which was what she did when she was determined not to let herself cry.

"It just didn't work, was all," Sarah said, like she was trying to make me feel better about it. And Nora had told Sarah?

"I'm sorry," I said. "I wish you had told me."

"I didn't want you to be sad for me," Nora said. "And anyway, it doesn't matter now. This last batch stuck."

"Batch?"

"You know the way it works. They put in half a dozen or so eggs, then you wait and see how many of them attach."

I guess I didn't know how it worked; I just had some vague ideas from scanning *Newsweek* articles in doctors' offices. Besides, my head was now too full of information: Nora had had two miscarriages; Nora was pregnant; Nora was pregnant with a batch. "What do you mean, 'How many of them'?"

"Well, one, probably. The greatest chance is for one. At least one."

"But you could have six?" I sat down on the arm of the sofa.

Nora smiled hugely, a smile so sweet and vacant, a smile so utterly unlike any expression I had ever seen on her face before, that I wondered if they had attached one of the fertilized eggs to her brain. "No one actually has six, except that woman who's always on the cover of *Good Housekeeping.*"

"I think she had seven," I said.

"Eight," Sarah said. "She had eight."

Nora laughed. "Well, we don't need to worry about that. All I want is one nice, healthy baby. That's what I'm going to concentrate on now."

I wanted to tell her that concentration had nothing to do with it, but there was no sense in getting into that.

Alex walked in from the kitchen eating a yogurt out of its little cup. He was wearing the same goofy smile that Nora had, the smile of someone who had hit the jackpot.

"I didn't know you were here!" I said, getting up to kiss him on the cheek. "Congratulations!"

"If you had known I was coming, you would have stocked in some real food." He scraped his spoon around the bottom of the cup.

"I'm the one who's supposed to be hungry," Nora said, sounding very much like the sunny heroine of a romantic comedy.

Alex was startled. "Are you hungry? There's really nothing in there but yogurt, but I can go out and get you something."

Nora reached up and squeezed his wrist. "Sweetheart, I'm kidding." She looked up at me, her eyes bright as new pennies. "Is he going to be the cutest father?"

"The cutest," I said. There was no other possible answer to such a question.

"Can we tell Romeo?"

"You could tell him, but he wouldn't hear you. The doctor gave him a shot. He's completely out of it."

"What are you going to tell Romeo?" Big Tony walked in with Sandy. He thought we were talking about his father's back because, of course, until a few minutes ago that was the big news of the day. His face was still sick with worry.

"We're going to have a baby!"

Big Tony and Sandy just stood very close together, looking puzzled. They reached down and locked their pinkie fingers. "But you don't want a baby," Sandy said finally.

"I do!" Nora said.

"But you hate babies. When I was pregnant—"

Nora cut her off. "That was a long time ago."

"It wasn't such a long time—Sarah, you have got to turn that movie off!"

I have to say, I had risen above *Wonka* for a moment. I didn't even hear him.

Sarah looked up at her mother from the safe custody of her aunt's arm. "We can't turn it off, now that she's going to have a baby. This means it's working."

"It doesn't mean that the movie is working. It means that nature is working, or it means science is working. Besides, no one can watch television for their entire pregnancy." Sandy glanced around for the clicker, but Sarah deftly slipped it under her thigh, so Sandy walked over and turned the television off. We were all startled by the sudden silence of the room.

Sarah took in a deep breath to begin her Wonka-deprived caterwauling, but Sandy turned on her quickly. "Don't start. Not now. We're going to have one adult moment in this family without singing chocolate bars."

"They don't *sing*," Sarah said, implying that her mother had lost her mind.

Sandy opened her mouth to say something, but nothing came out. She stood there for a minute, guppylike, opening and closing and coming to nothing. Sarah was so struck by the sight that she forgot to cry, and instead Sandy burst into tears.

"I'm sorry," Sandy said. "It's just such good news. It caught me off guard. I shouldn't be so emotional. I'm really happy—" She turned and walked out of the room and went upstairs.

Alex clapped Big Tony on the shoulder. "We've been crying all day. That's what babies do to people, I guess."

"I guess," Tony said weakly.

I slipped off the couch and followed Sandy up to her room, the room that had been hers when she was a baby and a little girl and a teenager and a single mother coming home and a married woman. I remembered putting together the crib with Mort, then taking it apart to bring in a toddler bed; then there were two twin beds so her friends could sleep over. She got the double bed after her divorce. I thought that *I* hadn't gotten very far away from where I started out, but Sandy hadn't even moved across the hall. I tapped on her door, then let myself in. Sandy never could hear anything when she was crying.

I sat down beside her on the bed and stroked her marvelous confusion of hair. "What is it?"

"Nora hates babies."

"I know. I guess her biological clock just caught up with her."

Sandy rolled over on her back and wiped her pillowcase across her eyes. "She always made me feel so bad about myself. She had this big career and all this money, and I was home with my kids. She acted like I was such a failure."

"Nora never thought you were a failure," I said. I had to say it, but I didn't know that for sure. It seemed perfectly possible.

"Now she gets to have a baby. Even Dad and Lila get to have a baby. Sometimes I feel like everybody gets a baby except me."

"Well, you've had two babies."

Sandy covered her eyes with her hands and started crying in earnest. I had to wait awhile before she could even breathe clearly. "I want another one!"

"You want to have another baby?" Was that possible? Her children could pour their own breakfast cereal and take their own baths. They knew how to program the VCR. Who would want to go backward from that?

"I want to have a baby with Tony. But we can't. There isn't any money, and he's back in school, but Nora can just snap her fingers and get to have anything she wants."

I lay down next to Sandy and let her cry in my arms. I didn't know what to say to her: that two children were plenty, and you didn't need to have a baby with someone to really love him, and that Nora had tried really hard to get pregnant. But sometimes a mother is just a box of Kleenex, silent and comforting, a willing place for a girl to pour out her sorrows.

Chapter Five

AFTER KNOWING EACH OTHER IN A LIMITED AND inaccurate context for most of our lives, Romeo and I started dating three years ago. *Dating* is a very thin word. It calls up images of malt shops and hand holding, which gives some indication of the last time I dated. These days Romeo was my business partner, my dear friend, my paramour. He was not, however, my husband or the man I lived with.

This had something to do with the fact that his ninety-three-year-old mother, his son Alan, Alan's wife Theresa, their three children, and their children's dog, Junior, were living with him, just as my daughter Sandy, Romeo's son Big Tony, and Sandy's two children, and their cat, Oompah-Loompah, lived with me. At one point we had actually discussed the possibility of moving all the children into Romeo's house and Romeo and I living together in my house. It wouldn't make anything more expensive, but logistically it wouldn't work in terms of everyone having bedrooms.

For awhile we managed to keep a tiny studio apartment so we'd have someplace where we could go and be alone, but times were tight, and after a year of struggling to keep two flower shops open and employ all our children, we had to give it up.

We didn't do sleepovers. I suppose we could have; these were modern times; but we both felt too weird about it with all the kids in the house. Children have a tendency to throw up in the middle of the night. They have bad dreams. And when they stumbled out of bed at 3:00 A.M., nauseated or frightened or both, they didn't differentiate between Mama's door and Grandma's door, they just came in.

So even though Romeo and I lived completely intertwined lives and spent our days together at work and caught the blessed and rare moment alone to make love, we virtually never went to sleep together in the same bed unless we managed a rare, tiny weekend vacation up in Maine.

Now here I was, exhausted from what had been by any standard a day of enormous importance, standing at the foot of my own bed.

And Romeo, the man I longed to go to bed with, was as comatose as Juliet in her tomb.

Sarah and Little Tony had gone to sleep with no questions about where I was planning to sleep or when Romeo was going home. They seemed to understand that he was sick and staying over, and no one so much as batted an eyelash. I was clearly not creating a situation that would keep them tied up in therapy through their middle years.

I sat down on the edge of the bed. Romeo was unmovable on the side I thought of as my side, the side that had been Mort's side back in the days Mort slept in this bed. I unlaced my sneakers and pushed them off, but kept the rest of my clothes on. I had learned that lesson, at least. I slipped beneath the covers fully dressed and carefully, carefully, so as not to create the slightest bit of bounce, leaned over and kissed my true love's cheek.

"Good night, Romeo," I whispered. There was not a flicker of response, and for a minute I placed my hand on the side of his neck to make sure that everything was still okay.

That night, I dreamed I was hugely pregnant. I was beside myself with worry, and I paced the floor wearing a green dress that looked like a pup tent. "Romeo, what have we done?" I said. "We're too old for this. We'll be eighty when the baby goes to college."

But Romeo didn't seem to be concerned. "Everything will be wonderful," he said, his hands on my belly.

"But we can't!" I wailed. "It isn't right. Who'll take care of the baby if we die?"

"We have big families. There's plenty of love to go around. There will be plenty for our baby."

And the very next minute, since this is the way things go in dreams, the baby was in my arms, all wrapped up tight in a white blanket. It was a little boy, my first son, and I felt that rush of happiness I had felt only twice before in my life, the perfect moment of complete possibility and goodness. There was never such a beautiful baby as this child, this bundle of light. I cried over his fine black hair and fat cheeks. "Romeo, look. Look at our son!"

Romeo took the baby high over his head and shook him gently, and the baby laughed and laughed. "And you thought it was too late!"

I held on to his arm, nearly drowning in all the love I felt for these two. *I am Charlie Bucket. I found the golden ticket.*

When I woke up it was the middle of the night, and I was holding on to Romeo's arm, my whole body pressed in tight to his.

"What is it?" he said sleepily.

"I woke you up. I'm sorry." I touched his forehead. "Are you okay?"

"My back hurts," he said. "And I have twenty-four cotton balls in my mouth."

I sat up and turned on the light beside the bed. He looked impossibly tired for someone who had been sleeping so hard. "I'll get you some water and a pain pill. Tony went out and had your prescriptions filled."

"He's a good boy." Romeo's voice sounded like it was being excavated one word at a time from the darkest recesses of his chest.

I moved carefully away from him and got the pill and the cup, but when I came back he only looked at me. "I don't know about this," he said. He drew in his elbows and tried to push up, then he made a sound that was something like, "Ike!" and put his arms down again. His head had not left the pillow a quarter inch.

"It's okay," I said, realizing that there were some advantages to having young children in your house. I went very quietly down to the kitchen and brought up the box of bendy-necked straws that Sarah demanded when drinking chocolate milk. I also picked up a long narrow vase just in case a trip to the bathroom could not be arranged.

"You're a very thoughtful person," Romeo said.

I held down the straw. "I'm a mother. It comes with the territory."

"I'm not going to be awake much longer," he said, when I

slipped into bed. "Is there anything going on that I should know about?"

"I feel pretty awful about your back," I said.

"Don't."

"Oh, and the big news is that Nora's pregnant and thrilled, and Sandy is devastated because she and Tony want to have a baby, and they can't afford one."

Romeo gave a small smile. "Then I'm happy for Nora and sorry for Sandy." He looked like he might have said more on the subject but it took too much energy, and he was on his way back to sleep.

I leaned over and put my head on the corner of his pillow. It was so wonderful and strange to have Romeo in my bed, and everything in me wanted to wrap myself around him. "Romeo?"

"Hm?"

"Do you ever wish we'd had a baby together?"

"We had plenty of babies."

"But do you think it would have been nice? Not that it could have happened; it's too late."

"No," he said.

In my dream you were so happy, I wanted to say to him, *you were crazy about our baby.* But all I said was, "Oh."

"Having babies was a lot of work," he said drowsily. "I like it better this way." He yawned. "If I had known how nice life could be without babies, I would have told Camille we weren't having any."

I closed my eyes and watched Romeo toss our baby up in the air again, but this time the wind caught the baby, and he blew straight up into the night and disappeared into the stars. My fat baby flew away from me, and, much to my surprise, I was still perfectly happy. I allowed myself the pleasure of putting one hand lightly over Romeo's wrist and together we fell back to sleep.

It was just barely light when the phone started ringing. Romeo opened one eye, then closed it. I started to reach over him to get the phone, but then I thought better of it. I got out of bed and walked around.

"Julie?" a man's voice whispered.

"Yes?"

"It's Alan. Tony told me that Dad hurt his back again."

"Oh, Alan, I'm sorry. I should have called you. Things were a little hectic around here last night."

But the truth was more complicated. I didn't feel comfortable calling Romeo's sons. I never had quite gotten over how much they had hated me at first. Even though they were perfectly nice to me now, Big Tony and Plummy, Romeo's daughter, were the only two I felt completely at ease with.

"No, no, that's not a problem. It's just that Grandma's been waiting up all night, and she's pretty confused. Theresa can't get her calmed down. I told her that Dad was staying with a friend, but she didn't believe me."

"Who's on the phone?" I heard the old woman bark out in the background.

This was perhaps the single most compelling reason why Romeo and I didn't live together: his rotten mother. Though his sons had come to peace with me, his mother still believed I would best be dispatched with a silver bullet through my heart. Candidly, I figured she was bound to die pretty soon and that I might as well sit tight and wait her out. But at ninety-three she seemed suspiciously healthy; only her mind had gone. It seemed to me she was mostly living in the 1950s, at the very height of her family hating my family. I figured her plan was to outlive me so as to deny me any chance of greater happiness. I both admired Romeo for honoring his pledge to take care of the old bat and cursed him for not putting her in a home. Not that we could have afforded a home. Alan's wife Theresa, a sainted, silent Italian girl, stayed home and took care of the senior Mrs. Cacciamani, her own three children, and Junior, the dog.

"Your dad's pretty doped up," I told Alan, "but let me see if I can wake him."

There was a ruckus on the other end of the line. "Is that Romeo you're talking to? Give me the phone!"

"Grandma, it isn't Dad. Let go of the cord."

I waited for Alan to say no, don't wake Dad up, but instead he said, "Yeah, I think that would be best."

I gave Romeo a gentle tap right in the middle of his chest. It wasn't even six o'clock in the morning. "Hey, Romeo, hey, wake up."

He opened his eyes enough to squint at me. "Is something wrong?" he said. I could tell the cotton balls were back.

"Here, take a sip of water and talk to Alan on the phone. Your mother is worried about you." I would not have said this so nicely were it not for the fact I knew Alan could hear every-thing. I held down the bendy-neck straw, and Romeo took a long drink. Then I held the phone next to his ear.

"Alan?" He stopped and cleared his throat, struggling to make his voice sound more awake. "No, I'm fine, my back is fine. Just a little catch. I'll be completely fine. Put Mom on the phone, I'll talk to her." Romeo waited, looked up at me, mouthed the words "good morning." "Mom? Yeah, it's me. . . . No, I'm great, I just stayed over with a friend. . . . I went to Mass, I did. I saw Father Al yesterday."

As I listened to Romeo lie, some deeply insane part of me wanted to say, why won't you tell your demented ninety-three-year-old mother that you're with me? How will she ever learn to accept me if you pretend like we're not together? Mentally, I gave myself a good slap and got over it.

". . . No, I won't miss work. I didn't stay up too late. How are you feeling this morning? . . .Well, I'm sorry I kept you up. Mom, I've got to get going now. . . . That's right, I have to go to work. . . . I love you, too. Don't be too hard on Theresa. Do what she tells you to do. Let me talk to Alan again."

When Alan got back on the phone, Romeo told him to call if there were any problems at work.

"And what?" I said when I hung up for him. "You'll come right over?"

"I might be helpful over the phone," he said.

"That's true, but you can't pick the phone up."

"I can pick you up, and you can pick the phone up."

"You do realize your back is broken, don't you? This isn't a catch."

"I compressed some vertebrae. It's hardly a broken back."

"It's a break in a bone in your back."

"That's a very small technicality."

I smiled. "Listen to us arguing. We're finally living together."

"It was the only way I could think of to weasel my way into your house so you wouldn't throw me out."

"You know, I think I won't go into work today. I think I should stay home with you."

"Oh no," Romeo said.

"Really, Tony and Sandy can manage one store, and Alan and Raymond will cover the other one. They'll be fine. How often do I get to spend the day alone with you?"

"What a sad waste. A day in the house alone with you, and all I can do is stare at the ceiling and swallow pain pills."

"Our relationship isn't built entirely on sex. It's mostly built on sex, of course, but we're perfectly capable of talking, too."

"I'll look forward to it."

In retrospect, this was a very funny conversation. Did I really think that going to work was a possibility? Romeo could only move his arms. Probably he could hold a piece of the newspaper, carefully prefolded, directly above his face and read it. He could hold a glass that was handed to him, but really, that was about it. He needed me, and I do not mean that in the romantic sense of, "Oh, he *needs* me." I mean that the man I love had just about the same ability to look after himself as a six-week-old baby.

"I'm going to take a quick shower," I said.

"That's great. If I could just get one more pill from you before you go?"

How could I have forgotten the pill? I fumbled with the childproof top, which took a little bit of muscle to push down and turn, a complete impossibility for the back-injured. "I'm so sorry! It's right here." I dropped one down his open gullet and held the straw near his mouth.

He swallowed and gave a weak smile. "And one more thing, I hate to ask . . ."

"Anything."

"If I could just brush my teeth."

"Of course."

"I didn't brush them last night and, well . . ."

"I'll go get the equipment."

I ran into the bathroom and looked under the sink in the big shoe box where I keep things like extra toothbrushes, where I always had extra toothbrushes, where there were no extra toothbrushes to be found. I picked up my own pink Oral-B, which was ever so slightly frayed around the outer bristles, and considered the limitations of love. I held it under hot running water, put on some toothpaste, picked up another glass, and strolled brightly into the bedroom.

"I think I can do this," he said. I handed him the brush,

hoping that no questions would be asked. He guided it very gingerly toward his mouth. Then he swiped the brush gently over the surface of the enamel, wincing slightly from time to time. He was dusting his teeth, not scrubbing them.

"Do you want me to do that?"

He spoke carefully, his mouth full of toothpaste, and little clumps of foam formed at the corners. "It's just that the back ones are a little far away right now."

I picked up the brush and went in. I have brushed plenty of teeth in my day that were not in my own mouth. I pulled up his lip with one finger and went up and down. I told him to open, to stick out his tongue, to take a drink of water from the bendy straw and spit.

But we had not properly accounted for the spitting. After a few swishes he just looked at me, his cheeks blown out and his lips bunched tight. He looked like an unhappy blowfish waiting for guidance. Spitting involved sitting up, or else one of those suction devices the dentists slip into the side of your mouth that were strong enough to vacuum out your fillings. I didn't have one of those.

"Okay," I said, "one second." I ran back into the bathroom, grabbed two hand towels, and stuffed one on either side of his neck. "Spit it up."

He just looked at me. I could tell he was thinking about swallowing. "If you swallow, it will just make you sick. Now spit."

His eyes turned back toward the glass, and he pointed. I wasn't sure what he wanted. "The glass?" He closed his eyes. "The straw?" And his eyes brightened. I stuck the straw between his lips and he blew the toothpaste liquid back into the glass, proving once and for all that he was a genius.

"That was a low point," he said.

"Do you want me to floss?" I meant it as a joke, though I realize there is nothing particularly funny about flossing.

"Would you?" he said, his voice welling with tenderness and disbelief.

There was not a shower for me after all. Once the teeth were clean there were bathroom issues to address, then a careful sponge bath. I had a pair of white cotton pajamas with tiny pink roses on them, roses so tiny that they might have passed for pink footballs if you didn't look too closely, and with some real effort I was able to get him into those.

Then he admitted he was hungry, having missed dinner last night and, honestly, lunch as well, and a cheese omelet would be perfect with some buttered wheat toast. We both agreed that cereal on one's back would be pretty much out of the question; and a cup of coffee, if it was just warm and wouldn't melt the straw, would make all the difference in the world. I couldn't have been happier to do it, and he couldn't have been nicer in asking.

"Wow, we're having omelets for breakfast?" Little Tony said, setting his pile of school books down on the kitchen table.

I did not miss a beat. "That's right," I said, heading back to the refrigerator for more eggs. There was time. Romeo wasn't going anywhere. I neatly folded the one I had in the pan and slid it onto the plate, and gave it to Tony tucked between four neat triangles of toast.

Little Tony looked at his plate, then looked at me. He blinked. "Wow," he said again, though this time it was softer.

Sarah made her entrance into the kitchen just as the second one was coming up, and though I needed to get upstairs, I couldn't see how I could make an omelet for her brother, then point her toward the cereal box. I set the second one down in front of her.

She picked up her fork and very gently touched the top to see if it was real. "Thank you," she said. No sarcasm, no jokes.

The children were so touched, so nearly speechless at the sight of a hot meal in the morning, that I felt like I had been a seriously bad grandmother indeed. It wouldn't kill me to send them out into the cold world with something more sustaining than a bowl of Cheerios under their tiny belts.

"Grandma, are you going to the grocery store today?" Sarah asked casually.

I seemed to wind up at the grocery store nearly every day of my life. It called to me like upstream called to a salmon. I asked her what she needed.

"Just a lottery ticket. Just one. I need a Big Game Mega Millions."

Her brother rolled his eyes. "Why don't you ever play the Mass Millions? The odds are better."

"It's small-time," she said.

"It's 7 million dollars."

"Mega Millions is 47 million. You aren't very good at math."

"I'm better at math than you are."

"Kids, please," I said. I poured more eggs into the still-hot pan.

Sarah pushed a slip of paper in my direction. "I wrote my numbers down."

"Everybody knows your numbers," Tony said.

"I told your mother I wouldn't buy you any more tickets," I said. "Besides, Nora just got you a dozen."

"They were quick picks. They weren't my numbers."

I had planned to be firm in my resolve, but when Big Tony walked into the room I snatched up the slip of paper and stuck it in my pocket, not wanting him to see that we were even discussing it. It wouldn't be the end of the world if I bought her one more. It was only a dollar, after all.

Big Tony had appeared at the very moment omelet number three was flopped onto the plate. His timing was so flawless I had to wonder if he hadn't been pushed from the wings by some unseen stagehand. I was feeling less sanguine about the whole egg preparation business. His plate hit the table with something of a clatter while I picked up the children's dishes and ferried them back to the sink. I went back to the refrigerator and took the last two eggs from their cardboard nest. Inappropriately, I thought of Nora, so many eggs. Sandy rushed into the room in a flurry of getting ready to go but she stopped, hopeful, and said, "Eggs?"

I am ashamed to say I raised my butter knife. "No! I only have two left, and they're not for you."

"Bad night?" she said, artfully lifting one eyebrow. She quickly assembled the kids' peanut butter sandwiches, folding over one piece of slathered bread and eating it for breakfast while she worked.

The coffee had reached lukewarm perfection as I managed one last omelet, this one low on cheese but perfectly rendered. I put a place mat and cloth napkin on a cookie sheet, the way the girls used to do for me on Mother's Day when they were tiny. I was taking Romeo breakfast in bed for the first time since we had been together, and damn the circumstances, I wanted it to be nice. I had the eggs, the toast, and coffee, a miniature glass of juice, the salt and pepper shakers. In a perfect world there would have been a single rosebud in a vase, but if the cobblers' children had no shoes, the florists' certainly had no flowers.

Sandy had applied grape jelly to bread and sealed the sandwiches in their plastic bags and paper bags. She looked at the clock in panic.

"I don't want to leave you with such a mess," she said.

"It's my mess. Go. You're a sweet kid. Tomorrow I'll cook you breakfast."

She leaned over and kissed me, then in another minute she had marshaled the troops out the door. Sarah turned back and waved good-bye. Then she winked at me, just like Shirley Temple.

I left the dishes behind and sailed up the stairs on a cloud of good intentions. I would sit beside my love and cut up the eggs held together by yellow cheese, and feed them to him one bite at a time.

"I'm sorry it took me so long, but there were some kids who cut ahead of you in line," I said.

But no one said anything back.

"Romeo?"

Eat first, then the pain pill—that was the lesson I learned for the future. Romeo and his clean teeth were out cold, and there would be no waking him. I wanted to show him what I had done, the heartbreaking sincerity of food on a tray. But then I realized there would be more food on more trays in the very near future, and I set the tray down on the floor and ate.

Chapter Six

SINCE THE BEGINNING OF TIME, MOTHERS HAVE tried to figure out how it is possible for something as small as a baby to create such a black hole in space. How does a mammal the size of an average Jack Russell terrier generate six loads of laundry a day? How is it possible that their slightest discomfort can wipe out every trace of logic, forcing you to call your pediatrician at 3:00 A.M. to report the fact that your baby is sniffling? How can they take every ounce of your mental and physical energy when they can't scoot two inches on their own?

When I was pregnant with Nora I bought French tapes, thinking that since I had all this time at home, I could finally master the language that had earned me a *C* my junior year of high school. In fact, the reality of motherhood left no time for vocabulary words and the conjugation of irregular verbs whatsoever. Once my baby was born, I felt a shining sense of accomplishment the weeks I managed to lug the trash out to the curb.

Having a man with a compressed vertebra in my bed proved not so dissimilar an experience. There was no squalling, of course, and it was a real time saver to have him be able to tell me what he wanted when he wanted it, but other than that, I was working like crazy to keep up. I was up and down those wicked stairs a hundred times a day, taking up sandwiches and heating pads and ice packs and various pills, bringing down trays and plates and glasses and finished crossword puzzles and bundles of wash.

"You're a real angel," he said to me, staring up at my ceiling.

Yeah, yeah, yeah, I wanted to say, feeling cranky and tired. "It's not a problem." Then I leaned over and kissed his forehead.

When, on the fifth day after what I thought of as Romeo's "accident," my need to complain started to feel reckless, I did what any sensible woman would do: I took the cordless phone outside, sat down on the chilly back steps that overlooked my garbage cans, and called my best friend. With Gloria I was free to wallow in self-pity for as long as I wanted, without having to endure the unpleasant aftertaste of guilt that comes from making a scene.

"Do you still love him?" Gloria asked.

I sighed, exasperated. It was such a trick of Gloria's, throwing out an impossibly worst-case scenario to defuse the crisis at hand with perspective. "Of course I still love him. I probably love him more."

"You're just tired," she said.

"Very tired."

"And you aren't having any sex."

"It's a privilege I lost once I broke his back."

"It wasn't your fault."

"I didn't see anybody else there."

"So this is penance?"

Penance. I hadn't thought of it that way. It was a very Catholic concept. Was it possible that all my work was simply paying off the damage I had done?

"I guess that could be it. I'm not saying Romeo is asking me to do all the things I'm doing. Most of it comes from me. He really tries very hard not to be too demanding."

"When Buzz had his heart attack, he started asking me to cut the crusts off his sandwiches. He told me he wanted to drink mango juice in the morning. He said he had to have ESPN on, even when he was asleep."

"Oh God, it's nothing like that." I looked around to make sure that no one was within earshot. "Maybe I'm just frustrated because having him around makes me realize how much I wish

I did live with him." I hadn't admitted this to Romeo. I hadn't even really admitted it to myself. Despite the constant running around, I really liked having him there. I wanted to keep him.

"I guess you could always compress another one of his vertebrae."

"No, seriously. With Sandy and Tony and the kids and all of Romeo's family, sometimes I think this is the only chance we're ever going to have to live together. It makes me feel . . . I don't know—"

"Wistful."

"Exactly." Gloria had an annoying habit of finishing my sentences but sometimes she did a better job of it than I would have, anyway.

"Speaking of Sandy and the kids, tell Sarah I'll drop her lottery tickets by sometime tomorrow."

"Her lottery tickets?"

"She called and asked me to pick them up for her. She said everybody at home was so busy with Romeo that she didn't want to bother anyone. Isn't that cute? She's so grown-up on the telephone."

"How many did she ask you for?"

"Just two," Gloria said. "But I got her three. They're only a dollar."

"Sandy told us . . ." I started, but then I saw there really wasn't any point.

"Don't worry about Sandy. You should be concentrating on Romeo. The man you love is helpless in your bed. Seize the day!"

Living with a person changes things. After three years of feeling very close to Romeo, I suddenly realized I had never really known him at all. You may think you speak the language, but until you actually live in the country you're just playing around. Romeo liked hot things hot and cold things cold. Plenty of ice in everything, including orange juice. He liked to watch the *Today Show* in the morning and seemed particularly smitten with the wide-eyed female host, though he denied it. He preferred the *Times* to the *Globe,* slept in socks, and hummed along with any piece of Beethoven that came on the radio. He woke up cheerful in the morning, even when under the influence of various pharmaceuticals. He slept with his mouth wide-open at night but did not snore.

But the main thing I came to realize about Romeo was that he was a very popular guy. All day long, the doorbell rang. Dominic came first thing in the morning and often showed up again on his way home from work. During the early visit (and I do mean early; he often arrived just after six) he always comported himself in a very doctorly fashion, asking Romeo questions about his pain levels, moving his arms and legs around, and listening to his heart.

"Why are you listening to his heart?" I asked, somewhat alarmed in my fuddle of sleepiness. "Is there something wrong with his heart, too?"

Dominic folded up the stethoscope and shrugged. "Just a habit."

When Dominic returned in the evenings, after the dinner dishes were loaded into the dishwasher, Romeo's back never seemed to cross his mind. He just sat on the edge of the bed drinking a gin and tonic, talking about baseball.

"Who talks about baseball in October?" I asked Romeo.

"Dominic thinks that's when the real game is going on. People get lined up for trades. Decisions get made that affect the whole next season."

Often Father Al would come along with his brother, either in the morning or at night, and pull up the little chair beside the bed and give Romeo communion whether he wanted it or not. If for some reason he missed his ride with Dominic, he showed up alone later on. "I just thought I should check in on him," he'd say almost sheepishly when I opened the door.

There seemed to be a certain sense of competition between the two brothers over who got more of Romeo's attention, in the same way there seemed to be a bit of jockeying among Romeo's sons, who dropped by in a continual stream. One would just be waving good-bye and here came another one marching up the stairs, like guards at Buckingham Palace swapping off their watch. Did they worry about leaving him alone with me too long?

Raymond, the only single Cacciamani son, brought over his digital camera and held it directly over his father's face to show him pictures of the different floral arrangements he'd made that day. "I'm really moving the little sweetheart roses," he said. "The supplier messed up and sent us a double shipment this week, so I'm putting them in everything."

"That's good," Romeo said, trying to be encouraging. "The pink bouquets look nice."

"They look like springtime." Raymond took the camera back and peered into the little screen. "Springtime in October. Not bad."

I leaned in to take a look. I wasn't at the stores any more than Romeo was, and I was anxious to get any little visual clue of what was going on. "How are the mums moving?"

Raymond scrolled quickly through his pictures and showed me a sea of potted mums near the front door of Roseman's. He had clumped all the colors, whites with the whites, pinks with pinks, yellows with yellows, then pressed all the clumps in close together, raising some up on bricks to change the height. It looked like a float, like a massive flower arrangement on the floor.

"Raymond, that's beautiful." I was genuinely moved.

"Don't worry," he said, showing me another shot taken from outside so I could see how nicely the mums showed from the sidewalk. "We've got everything under control."

Alan, who lived at Romeo's and also worked in the stores, brought over his three children, Tommy, Patsy, and Babe. He told them they were not to bounce on the bed. They moved around Romeo very carefully, touching his nose, kissing his wrists.

"Does it hurt very much?" Tommy asked.

"Not much," Romeo said. "It only hurts when I yawn."

"Junior ate the Halloween pumpkin," Babe said. She was a dreamy little girl of five with straight black hair cut into a pixie. "And it isn't even Halloween yet."

"We'll get you a new pumpkin," I told her.

Patsy eyed me with sudden suspicion. "Where's your room?" she asked, as if she had just done the math in her head.

"I take naps on the couch," I said. "I don't need a whole lot of sleep."

Pretty soon they all wandered back down to the living room

to see Sarah, who had suggested it would be very nice if they all watched *Willie Wonka* together since they were practically cousins or something. When I went downstairs later I found the three little Cacciamanis lined up in a neat row in front of the television with my granddaughter.

"Where's your father?" I asked.

Tommy unglued himself from the story long enough to speak a sentence. "He said we could stay and spend some time with Grandpa."

And so I inherited three more children for dinner.

It wasn't as if all of Romeo's boys were around. His son Nicky was in the Air Force and still stationed in Germany, so he didn't come by at all. But Big Tony made up for his absence by being around all the time. All of his latent desires to be a doctor unleashed themselves on Romeo. He was forever checking his father's pulse and looking into his eyes. "Enough with the penlight," Romeo said gently.

Tony read up on compression fractures on the Internet, and after the first week he put together a series of exercises that involved lifting Romeo's legs up and down to keep him from getting blood clots. Tony could be overly zealous, but he was unquestionably helpful when it came time to bathe and dress Romeo, and he did a lot of the cajoling it took to get Romeo on his feet for a minute or so every now and then as Dominic suggested. I didn't like to be the one to drag Romeo out of bed. The screwed-up look of pain on his face broke my heart.

The other son was Joe, the oldest, and whenever he came by I made myself especially busy in the kitchen. I had never quite forgotten the singular intensity with which he had tried to break Romeo and me apart during our early courtship, and while he was completely polite to me now, I remained secretly wary. Joe ran a trucking company, and everything about him was trucklike: He was big and solid and deliberate. I could swear I caught a slight hint of diesel in the wake of air he left behind him.

On the tenth day of Romeo's internment in my bedroom the doorbell rang—an unusual sound, as most of the visitors came so regularly they had taken to letting themselves in. I was upstairs folding laundry on the foot of the bed and talking to Romeo, who had just woken up from a long pain-pill nap, about whether or not we should wait until Thanksgiving to set up our Christmas displays, when all the other stores were already stringing up lights at Halloween. I heard Sarah yelling at Tony that she would get the door, but she sounded a little half-hearted. Doorbells were not nearly so interesting now that so many people came over all the time.

"Hi, Mr. Cacciamani. Hi, Mrs. Cacciamani."

"Hi there, Sarah," I heard Joe say. "Is my father upstairs?"

"Sounds like you've got company," I said to Romeo.

"It's about time someone came to see me," he said tiredly.

"He doesn't go anywhere," Sarah said from downstairs.

I was glad that Joe had brought his wife. I thought she lent a nice counterbalance to her husband's essential thuggishness. Nancy taught math at a Catholic school on the other side of Somerville, and so her schedule didn't tend to be very flexible. I wondered if today was some obscure Catholic holiday I didn't know about, the Blessed Holy Feast Day of Saint Somebody. The calendar was teeming with them, and it seemed to me the Catholic schools were closed as many days as they were open.

I smoothed the covers over Romeo and ran my hand quickly over his hair.

"Straightening me up?" he asked.

"I want them to think I take good care of you." It was my intention to say a very short hello, then slip back down to the kitchen, telling myself I was being thoughtful by letting the family have a little time alone together. Maybe Nancy would want to come downstairs with me and drink coffee. I could ask her whether or not she thought Sarah needed a math tutor.

"Okay," Joe said. "Up you go."

"Why is he upstairs?" a shrill voice demanded. "Who put him upstairs?"

I looked at Romeo, who had gained enough mobility by this point to turn his head and look at me. I mouthed the word, "Who?" and he mouthed back to me, "My mother." He was pale, or perhaps he was just reflecting my own paleness back at me.

Thump, thump came the heavy footsteps, the slow and deliberate encroaching of doom. It was like a horror film. I was trapped in the bedroom, and something truly wicked was coming up the stairs. I opened the door a tiny crack and peered out with one eye. There they were, huffing and puffing up to the second floor in a pose that was not entirely unfamiliar to me: the scariest son carting the scariest mother up and up in his arms. Joe was much bigger than Romeo, and the old witch Cacciamani was, I am sorry to say, much smaller than me, and still I could see him struggling. His receding hairline was crowned in stars of sweat, and I thought I heard some wheezing.

What if he went down, too? What if I had to lay another Cacciamani in my bed and nurse them both back to health, while the old woman harped me to death? I felt a cold chill and shut the door.

Thump, thump. They came closer. There wasn't time to ask the logical questions: *What could Joe possibly be thinking of bringing her over here without calling first?* Or, *Do you think she knows where she is?* There was only time for one question, the big question, and I whispered, "What are we going to do?"

"Hide," he said.

Without giving it a single thought, I stepped into my closet.

This was not a walk-in closet: This was a good, honest closet built for the good, honest sensibilities of the 1920s, when every man had three suits and every woman had four dresses and they could all be hung together without actually touching in a very small space. Whenever I opened my closet, I was confronted by the massive amount of superfluous junk that was crammed into it. My closet was a no-man's-land, a collection of things I had once needed and loved and had completely forgotten, horrible muumuus and corduroy jeans crammed in beside a couple of lovely cashmere sweaters. I stepped into a pool of my own shoes, bent down and shoved my shoulder into the densely packed wall of fabric, and pulled the door shut behind me. Had I stopped to give the whole situation two seconds of consideration, I would have been too late.

From inside my closet I heard the bedroom door swing open, somehow missing the knock that *surely* must have preceded an adult man bringing his grandmother over to see his father in his father's girlfriend's bedroom.

"Surprise!" Joe said in a weary voice.

"Put me down!"

"Hi, Ma," Romeo said.

"This is some hospital. Look at the junk that's lying around here."

"It isn't a hospital, Ma."

"I should say not. The nurses don't do anything for you. The one who let us in wouldn't even tell us your room number."

That's because she's eight years old, you idiot.

"Grammy, Dad's not in the hospital."

It was very snug inside my closet and very dark except for the small strip of light that came in from beneath the door. I was crouching on a pair of winter boots that were not altogether comfortable, but I was not unhappy in there. I realized I had probably never taken absolutely everything out of my closet and cleaned it, and as a result there was a certain amount of dust to contend with, but what did that matter? It was my stuff after all, and the smells were my smells, my perfume and my cedar blocks and the faint green odor of the flower shop that permeated my life.

And while many a woman might have been offended to have been asked to hide at the age of sixty-three in her own house, I was not. I felt saved from an impossible situation. Old woman Cacciamani might not be able to tell a bedroom from an intensive care unit, but I have no doubt she would have recognized me, and she would have wanted to know what in the hell Julie Roseman was doing in Romeo's hospital room.

"Why are you lying in bed?" she snapped. "I've already had lunch."

"I hurt my back," Romeo said patiently.

"Don't you remember, I told you about Dad's back. You've been asking where he was, so I brought you over here to see him." Joe's voice sounded huge and gruff, even when it was clear he was trying to speak gently to his grandmother. "See him? He's right there."

"Of course I see him. Do you think I'm blind? There's a cat on the floor. Even in Italy they didn't let cats into the hospital. It's not clean."

"Here, kitty-kitty-kitty," Joe said sweetly.

Oompah-Loompah meowed. "He went under the bed," the old woman said. "Disgusting."

"Everybody knows you've got good eyes, Ma," Romeo said, valiantly trying to change the subject. "Now tell me, are you being nice to Theresa?"

The saint, I thought at the very mention of her name. The one who stays home taking care of her children and her dog and her vicious ninety-three-year-old grandmother-in-law. I never understood the concept of Catholic sainthood until I met Theresa.

"That girl steals."

"Theresa doesn't steal, Ma."

"She takes my things. She takes my shoes."

"She picks things up," Romeo said. "She cleans up your room. If you want to know where something is, just ask her. She'll tell you."

I shifted my hips a quarter inch to the left, hoping to relieve the growing numbness in my legs, and in doing so must have stirred up some dust. And so I did what I always do in the face of dust: I sneezed. There wasn't any time to stifle it. It was an ambush sneeze.

"What was that?" the old woman said. A mind like a sieve but ears as sharp as a five-year-old's.

"Yeah, what was that?" Joe said curiously.

"Another patient," Romeo said calmly. "He's in the next room. Sneezes all day long."

"I want you out of here," Mother Cacciamani said. "The place is a pigsty. Look at this, leaving piles of laundry right here on your bed. How do you know if it's even clean? The germs in this place will kill you, and cats can smother you in your sleep. Whatever you've got now, it can't be as bad as what you could catch here."

"I'll come home as soon as I can," Romeo said.

"You can tell Joe to take you home with us." I imagined she

pointed up to the big man, thinking he could carry her to the car in one arm and take Romeo down in the other.

"No," Romeo said. "I should probably stay here just a little bit longer, at least until the doctor tells me to go home."

"Doctors don't know anything," his mother said. I thought I heard some sadness in her voice.

"Never as much as mothers."

"This place makes me tired," she said.

"Joe, why don't you take your grandmother home?"

"All right," Joe said with a heavy sigh.

"You could have at least stayed in a hospital that had an elevator. That wouldn't have been too fancy."

"You carried her up all those stairs?" Romeo said.

"And it looks like I'll be carrying her back down."

Romeo whistled, long and low. "You should watch your back, son."

Chapter Seven

ROMEO AND I MIGHT NOT HAVE BEEN LEGALLY married, but we were joined in the eyes of the law as business partners. We each owned half of the other's flower shop, both of which were now called "Julie and Romeo's." Still, it didn't exactly stick. Our customers never accepted the new names and flatly refused to use them.

Even when we talked about the stores, which we did incessantly, we always called his store Romeo's and we called mine Roseman's. We always said your store and my store. We didn't mean anything by it except as a means of differentiating: your store is low on birthday cards; I want to get some of those orchids over at my store. On the books we were profoundly conjoined, and because of that we got better prices on everything from long-stem reds on Valentine's Day to our accountant's fees.

There was also a great fluidity among our staff, because all of our staff now consisted of our children. If Big Tony was running deliveries for Roseman's, he'd call his brother Alan to see if there wasn't something that needed to go out at Romeo's. If Romeo's got backed up with arrangement orders, Raymond would call Sandy at Roseman's, and she would go over and lend a hand.

It was all a delicate balance, making sure that everybody got along and one store wasn't favored over the other, and Romeo and I sat at the helm of this great ship and charted the course. Calculating the profit margins in walk-ins and deliveries, the small gift items that could be real moneymakers, keeping on top of the distributors to make sure we were getting the very freshest product, the careful business of ordering just the right amount so that no one wound up with a store full of rotting tulips, was what we did. It worked because we made it work.

But then we stopped going to work, and instead of the world grinding to a halt the way we knew it would, everything moved forward with suspicious ease. Raymond, who had the most seniority and was the only one in his generation who looked at the shops as his career instead of his default source of employment, took over the managerial duties. When Romeo tried to grill him on the phone, Raymond gently blew him off. I stretched out next to Romeo in the bed, and he held the phone between our ears. After all, the stores did belong to both of us.

"Everything's fine, Dad. All you need to worry about is getting better."

"I AM getting better, and I'm coming back to work soon. I just want to know about the hydrangeas."

This wasn't exactly true. After a little more than two weeks Romeo could sit up and stand, but only for a few minutes. The rest of the time he was still flat on his back, eating Percocet.

"What's there to know?" Raymond said. "They're here, they're blue, they're beautiful."

"But who's doing the arrangements? You and Sandy can't be handling everything yourselves."

"We're okay."

"You aren't letting Tony do the flowers, are you?"

"You know I wouldn't do that."

A look of real horror passed over Romeo's face. "Not Alan!"

"Now you're just being silly," Raymond said calmly. He was quiet for a minute, but Romeo didn't say anything either. Then Raymond sighed, breaking the stand-off. "If you have to know, I'm bringing in a designer from New York, someone very chic. She's only going to work for a week or so, just until you're back."

I panicked. I started to say that we could never afford that, and then Romeo said it for me. "We don't have that kind of money."

"Dad, it's Plummy," Raymond said.

"Plummy's coming home?"

"She wanted to surprise you, so act surprised. She's taking some time off to come and see you, so I told her she might as well roll up her sleeves and help out."

"Do you really think she can spare the time?" Romeo's voice seemed small. "She's so busy now."

"Everyone else in the family works in these shops. I don't see why she can't."

"But it's Plummy," Romeo said.

"Can't you just pretend like you're on vacation? Pretend you're taking a cruise. Pretend that every phone call is ship-to-shore and is costing sixteen dollars a minute."

Romeo hung up the phone and turned his head to face me, a new trick he was really getting quite good at. "He doesn't need me."

"He needs you," I said.

"I can't believe Plummy's coming in to do our flowers."

"I know," I said, leaning my head gently against the side of his shoulder. "That really does defy imagination."

Having Plummy Cacciamani do the flowers in your neighborhood flower shop was a little bit like bringing in Meryl

Streep to star in the community theater production of *Carousel,* or hiring Lance Armstrong to teach your kid how to ride a bike. It was overkill.

At twenty-four, she was the youngest Cacciamani by many years and bore an eerie resemblance to Audrey Hepburn, with her enormous brown eyes and a neck like a willow branch. She had taken her degree in fine arts to New York City and within a year established herself as a floral artist. Not a florist, mind you. A Floral Artist. None of this calling up and ordering flowers nonsense.

People scheduled appointments with Plummy six months in advance. They booked their weddings and banquets and rooftop soirees around her packed calendar. They rushed her to the Hamptons and flew her to L.A. to consult about blossoms and twigs.

Her work, she said in one interview, was always informed by the space. She'd cover entire walls with thousands of forsythia branches flown up from Mississippi in March, bringing in teams of men to bind them down to her exact specifications, then she'd turn around and float a handful of cherry blossoms in a flat bowl of water. Her style transferred seamlessly from Japanese minimalist to full-throttle baroque depending on how she was moved.

And she was not above making sixteen-foot arrangements

loaded with roses and peonies, of the type one would see in the middle of the lobby of the Plaza Hotel, except hers always seemed like a parody somehow, an improvisation on a classic theme. The only thing consistent about her vision was its perfection.

As far as anyone could tell, no one had ever assembled plant life like Romeo's daughter, and her talent, coupled with her unnerving beauty and easy manner, made her a superstar in a field that had never had one before. Her name was linked to movie stars in the gossip column of the *Post*. She was the subject of a front-page profile in the Style section of the *Times*. And then, last spring, she was on the cover of *New York Magazine* holding a single daffodil over one eye. She was dubbed the It Girl of the season.

"Why can't Plummy help me with my Halloween costume?" Sarah complained, as I spread an ancient cake of blue eye shadow over her face. I had found it in the darkest corner of the bathroom linen closet, a cowering refugee from the early seventies.

"Because Halloween is in half an hour, and she's not coming until tomorrow."

"Maybe she could get here earlier."

"It's not going to happen," Sandy said, and brushed Sarah's hair hard until she got it all gathered up into a high ponytail.

Sandy had done a truly ingenious job on the costume, sewing a blue bed sheet onto a hula hoop so that Sarah was transformed, awkwardly, into a giant blueberry, just like that nasty little girl Violet in *Willie Wonka* who was punished for chewing too much gum. She wore blue tights, a blue turtleneck, blue mittens. She smacked blue gum.

"I don't think that Plummy could have come up with anything better than this anyway," I said, pulling a green stocking cap covered in large felt leaves down on her head. "There. You're a vision. Go show Romeo."

Sarah trudged through the hallway, her girth seeming sadly deflated. She lacked a certain puffiness, and I wondered for a minute if we should stuff her full of pillows. It would keep her warm, but it also might render her completely immobile. If only she had her own little team of Oompah-Loompah's to roll her from house to house.

"My bluebell!" Romeo said, lifting his head up off the pillow. "My star sapphire! My little robin's egg!"

"I'm a blueberry," Sarah corrected.

"I was getting to that one."

I felt sorry for Little Tony, who was suddenly too tall for costumes and candy. He seemed unfairly banished to adulthood, when I knew that all he really wanted was to tie a bandana on his head and put a paper patch over one eye and wear Sarah's old stuffed parrot on his shoulder. It was decided that he would take his little sister trick-or-treating, the logic being that most people would take pity on a too-tall boy and give him a couple of pieces of candy just for being a good sport.

"You'd think somebody would give out lottery tickets," Sarah said. "Even scratch tickets. It's always candy, candy, candy."

Sandy put a hand on either of Sarah's shoulders and looked her daughter in the face. "Sarah, you've got to snap out of this. We're going to have to start sending you to Gamblers Anonymous."

"I hear it's a great place to meet other third graders," I said.

"There's a drawing tonight," she said, as if she had ever given us the chance to forget. Then she tilted her head to one side, and gave a very knowing sort of nod. There was something about her blue skin that made her look less like a blueberry and more like a very wise alien. "I'm feeling very lucky."

"I don't know how you'd be feeling lucky, when I've told everyone to stop buying you tickets," Sandy said, tying a blue scarf around Sarah's neck. "Now go out into the night and beg strangers for candy."

Sarah waddled down the stairs and out the door into the cold wind, carrying an ambitiously oversized plastic bag from CVS. Little Tony trailed sullenly behind her, wearing jeans and a parka, his hands stuffed into his pockets. Big Tony followed them both at a discreet distance with a flashlight. They passed two ghosts and a blond toddler dressed as My Little Pony coming up the sidewalk. I gave out packages of M&Ms.

The plan was that Nora and Alex were coming over to help us hand out candy. They had never had a single child show up at their Back Bay condo, and while this had always been considered a plus in years past, now that Nora was pregnant she thought it was a tragedy. "I want to see what everybody's wearing," she had said. They were supposed to come before Sarah left so they could take pictures, but now it was well past dark, and they were still no-shows.

"She probably got busy at work," Sandy said. "She probably had to sell some mogul a house. Nora doesn't know a thing about making a promise to a child and keeping it."

The doorbell rang, and we doled out candy to a fireman and a kangaroo. I thought of Tony and slipped a little packet of candy to a young father who was lingering at the bottom of the stairs.

Sandy had stayed on the bitter side ever since receiving the news of her sister's pregnancy. It was as if Sandy had been the one who was pregnant, and Nora had somehow stolen it away from her.

"It could just be that she's late, you know," I told her.

"You can't be late when you have children," Sandy said.

I looked at her with deep incredulity, wanting to tick off every time she'd been late in the past week alone. "Sure you can."

Sandy stuck her hands deep into her curls and turned her head from side to side as if she was trying to screw it off her shoulders. It was a funny little thing she did when she got frustrated with herself. Even as a little girl, she would manually work her head back and forth when she did something stupid.

The doorbell rang again.

"Go upstairs with Romeo. I'll answer it," she said.

I felt like I should be able to be some sort of comfort to Sandy, but on the other hand I wanted to comfort Romeo, too. What I needed was some as-yet-uninvented product: a pressurized canister with which I could spray foamy comfort from room to room. Trying to comfort an entire house full of people manually was getting to be too much of a job. Sandy looked at me and pointed up the stairs. "Go," she said.

Romeo was sitting on the edge of the bed with his feet on the floor. He smiled at me.

"Look at you!" I said.

"It's progress. I'm almost ready to get out of here."

I sat down beside him and took his hand. "It's not as bad as all that."

He smiled. "Oh, Julie, if I were going to be held prisoner in anybody's bedroom, I'd want it to be yours." He did a small movement that was at once a turn and a lean forward. He was moving in to kiss me, but when his mouth came within two inches of mine, he screamed.

"What!"

Every muscle in his face tightened up. "Back down," he gasped. "Back down."

And so I helped him lie back and picked up his feet and very carefully stretched them out in front of him. I got him a pain pill and a glass of water with the bendy-neck straw. Someday, when he was ready, Romeo would go, but it wasn't going to be anytime soon.

When Dr. Dominic and Father Al showed up in a stream of cowboys and swamis and fifties girls in poodle skirts, I just pointed them up. They came back down five minutes later shaking their heads.

"I didn't think I'd have to spell this out for you, but stay away from all amorous activity," Dominic said. "No kissing."

After they left Sandy gave me a mildly horrified look. "What have you done now, Mother?"

But I had other things on my mind. Sarah and the two Tonys came back with their loot, and still there was no Nora, no Alex. I called them at home and on Nora's cell phone, but I didn't get an answer.

"She's going to miss the drawing." Sarah had taken off her blueberry husk and was now wearing only the blue tights, turtleneck, hat, and gloves. Every shade of blue was slightly mismatched. She looked like a little blue worm.

"The same numbers will come up if she's here or if she's home," Big Tony said logically. "Nothing's going to change."

But Sarah was a gambler and gamblers, especially the eight-year-old variety, are impervious to logic. "You don't know that," she said darkly.

Little Tony was going through the stash of candy in his pockets. He ultimately wound up with so much that at one point in the evening he had tightened up his belt and started dropping candy down the front of his shirt, so that now he wore a little potbelly of undigested sweets. "I got almost as much as Sarah did, and I didn't have to dress up like a blueberry."

Sarah switched the television on and sat back to peel a Starburst fruit chew. "Feeling very lucky," she said.

"I don't like this one bit," Sandy whispered to Big Tony.

I wondered if she didn't like it for the same reason that I didn't like it. It felt too scary to get caught up in the possibilities of Sarah's hope. With that kind of money, I could pay off the mortgage on the house and the one I should never have taken out on the store. Sandy could pay off her credit cards, and Big Tony could go to medical school, and they could all have a house of their own and go to private schools and take cello lessons and go to the Cape for two weeks in the summer.

With all that money, we would all be freed from all our financial worries. Think about all the time we'd have then. We'd never have to waste those hours feeling nervous over stacks of bills, and we'd never have to rush to make a matinee instead of going to the movies for full price in the evenings. We wouldn't have to pick one thing over another—not that we needed to have everything, but wouldn't it be lovely not to waste so much time trying to decide? Adults knew better than to allow themselves the luxury of pinning their hopes on crazy schemes, but watching Sarah do it, it was hard not to get swept away by the moment.

"Quiet!" Sarah said, though no one was talking. "This is it."

But it wasn't it. Ball after ball shot up and came to nothing. Even though she had managed to hustle eleven tickets from various sources, none of them had more than one of the numbers necessary to win.

Sarah stared at the television set after it was over, waiting for Dawn to come back on and say that she'd made a mistake, that she wanted to call the numbers again. "It's all Nora's fault," she said. "She promised she'd be here."

Sandy crouched down in front of her blue daughter and

brushed the loose springs of hair back with the flat of her hand. "It isn't Nora's fault, sweetheart. It's just bad luck."

"I'll win next week," Sarah said, in a voice so tired I wasn't even sure if she believed it herself. "Next week the jackpot will be bigger, and it will be even better to win then."

"There isn't going to be a next week for the lottery," Sandy said quietly. "This isn't the place you need to look for a golden ticket."

Sarah was crying a little, making muddied streaks in the eye shadow on her cheeks. Sandy picked her daughter up in her arms and carried her up the stairs like she was still a little girl, then washed all of the blue from her face and make her brush the candy out of her teeth before putting her in her bed.

Sandy was right about the bad luck. At eleven o'clock that night, Alex called from the hospital to tell me that Nora had started to bleed.

"She didn't lose the babies," he said. "She didn't want me to call you until we knew for sure, but the doctor says they're all still there. She's going to have to go on complete bed rest, but he thinks if she stays really still, she might be able to hold on to them."

"Them?" I said. "Alex, is Nora having twins?"

"Triplets," he said.

I was no stranger to counting to three. It was something I had managed easily even as a very young child, but now the skill completely eluded me. One and one and one. I couldn't make the numbers add up. I tried to see three babies in my mind, three babies sitting in a row, but each time I put that third one in the picture, the other two fell away. I couldn't even make myself *see* three babies, much less make myself think about what three babies would mean. I couldn't tell what was good luck and what was bad luck anymore. The two concepts had collided in my mind.

But for Sarah, the concepts were perfectly clear. The next morning it was announced on the radio that Kay Bjork from Stamford, Connecticut, had won the Big Game Mega Millions, all 234 of them.

"Be Jork?" Little Tony said. "What kind of a name is that?"

Sarah started to cry fat tears. "It isn't fair! It isn't fair! She isn't even from Massachusetts."

But the numbered Ping-Pong balls that blew up from the long, clear throat of the lottery machine knew no state loyalty. The pot, at least for the present moment, was again empty.

Chapter Eight

"I HAVE AN INCOMPETENT CERVIX," NORA SAID WHEN she called the next morning.

"Are you still in the hospital?"

"Do you think there's any insurance plan in this country that would allow me to stay overnight in a hospital for an incompetent cervix? They told me basically I wasn't allowed to walk until after the babies were born, and that I should see myself out."

"So what does this mean, exactly?"

"It means that my cervix is lazy. It's slothful."

"They called your cervix slothful?" I pictured a cervix that lay around the uterus all day smoking cigarettes, never picking things up.

"Maybe not in so many words, but you could tell that's what they were thinking: She has an indolent cervix, an insubstantial and unreliable cervix. Everything they said seemed very judgmental to me. Frankly, I don't think it's right. I'm forty years old, and I've never asked my cervix for anything. It's had a free ride all my life, and now that its moment has come, it's turned *faineant*."

"*Faineant?* I don't know that one."

"It's an irresponsible idler."

"That's a medical term?"

"No, actually, it's French."

My daughter was carrying triplets, and as long as they were the size of hairless mice, we could make jokes about how they were going to stay put, but once they got to be proper baby size, I could see that you'd want vigilance in a cervix.

"So what are you going to do?"

"Alex and I have been talking about it, and we both think it would be best if I came over there."

"Should you be riding around in a car? I can certainly come and see you."

"I thought about that, but you don't know how much longer Romeo is going to be stuck up on the second floor. It would be a hard time for you to leave."

"Don't be silly. I can leave."

Nora was quiet for a minute, then she made a little hiccupping sound.

"Nora?"

She was crying. "I just didn't know you'd be so great about everything."

"What are you talking about? Did you really think I wasn't going to come and see you?"

She sniffed, then inhaled sharply. "I'm sorry. It's all the hormones. I have four human beings worth of hormones coursing through my veins. It's just that, well, I know you weren't so crazy about the idea of my having a baby."

"That was before I understood that you actually wanted one."

"And so I imagined you'd be less than thrilled that I'm having three babies."

"We haven't even talked about that yet. I'm really not able to think in terms of three."

At this Nora laughed, and I laughed with her. "I just want to tell you I appreciate it. Your support, your help. You've been so nice about everything. The truth is I really do want to come over there, so that's that. Alex is going to drive me."

"You do whatever makes the most sense to you," I said, my voice brimming with motherly love. I was feeling good; I'll admit it. Nora and I didn't manage many warm moments and I was glad that she had turned to me and I had been there for her.

"We'll wait a couple of hours. I'm going to call now and have the hospital bed delivered."

"Hospital bed?"

"The doctor said they're a lot more comfortable for the long haul, being able to put your legs up and down, things like that. Have them put it in the living room, okay? I'm going to go tell Alex what to pack. I love you, Mom."

She hung up the phone and as soon as I heard that long dial tone, everything stopped. It stopped, and still I had the presence of mind to parrot back the sentence, "I love you, too," but she wasn't there to hear it. She was already packing to move home.

This is nothing a mother should admit, but I will say the happiest day of my life was the day that Nora left for college. The very fact that she was admitted into college with her wildly uneven grades, frequent delinquencies, and regular suspensions seemed like a miracle in itself. She scored in the top one percent on all the standardized testing and came up with a very poignant essay about choosing to walk away from a liquor store robbery that one of her boyfriends had encouraged her to participate in. That was enough to land her a spot at the University of Colorado.

She insisted on driving out in a U-Haul with a girlfriend, and Mort and I knew better than to argue. We stood there in the driveway as she pulled away, and I waved and looked sad, but really I was experiencing an enormous sense of lightness. Nora had gone off into the world. Nobody in the house was fighting. I went upstairs to take a nap and didn't wake up until noon the next day.

My life was transformed by Nora's absence, and for all I know, her life was transformed by my absence. When she crossed the Continental Divide, she managed to leave her old ways behind her. She was a new girl in the Rocky Mountain time zone. She arrived in Boulder a top-flight student, a mover and a shaker. Everything she touched was golden.

Why didn't I think that this was the girl who was moving back? The successful real-estate broker with the good marriage and the Kelly bag? Why did I think that if Nora spent the night in this house, she'd be that seventeen-year-old hellion again, the kind of girl who'd skip town and leave her mother to raise triplets?

I felt dizzy. I looked at my watch. A couple of hours, she said. Did that mean I had two hours left, or was she being loose with time? Could she have meant three or four? It didn't matter. I went upstairs to lie down.

Romeo was in bed with a set of headphones on, staring at the ceiling. When I came in the room he clicked off the tape player and smiled at me. "Al brought me *The Confessions of*

Saint Augustine on tape. He's been trying to get me to read it since we were in school. It's actually quite good."

I lay facedown on my pillow. "Nora's moving home."

"What?"

I turned my face to him. "Nora. She has a problem with her cervix, and she has to stay on complete bed rest until the triplets are born. She has to stay on complete bed rest, right here in my living room."

Romeo mulled over this information. How could he be sure about which part was so upsetting to me? Triplets? The possibility of losing triplets? The part about the living room? How could he know, when I wasn't completely sure myself?

He opted for the safe response. He told me he was sorry this was happening.

"Thank you," I said.

Romeo reached down and took my hand. "One day," he said, "we're going to go away to an island, just the two of us. And when we leave we won't tell anyone where we're going, and when we're there, we won't speak about any of our relatives at all. We'll still love them, but for a week or so we'll manage to forget about them completely."

"Will we drink margaritas and dance in the surf and make love every day at sunset?"

"Twice at sunset."

"Will this happen before or after the triplets are born?"

"I don't know for sure. It will depend on whether or not we're completely bankrupt by the time I get out of bed."

Downstairs I heard the doorbell ring, but I didn't care who it was. All I knew was that it was too soon to be Nora. I heard a brief flutter of voices, then feet on the stairs.

Sandy tapped on the door. "Mom? There are some men here who say they have a bed for us. Do you know anything about a bed?"

Nora, it seemed, had been planning on coming home all along.

Sandy moved in with me six years ago, when Sarah was two and Tony was six. She had meant to stay a couple of months, just until her divorce was final and she could get back on her feet. But nothing in life turns out the way we think it's going to, and instead of the three of them moving out, she married Big Tony and upped her number to four. I thought that because of the way her life had gone, she'd be sympathetic to the plight of her sister's cervix. I was mistaken.

"She can *hire* someone to take care of her in her own house. She doesn't need to come over here."

Two men wearing matching baseball caps and sweatshirts that said HOME HEALTH EQUIPMENT wrestled a monstrously large metal bed frame covered in gears and levers and different hydraulic contraptions, through my front door. It looked menacing, depressing. It was the kind of bed that made the neighbors think that hospice could not be far behind.

"Sandy, help me move a couple of chairs. We have to figure out where we're going to put this thing."

She locked her arms in front of her chest as if to say they were closed for business. "No." She sounded every bit like her eight-year-old daughter. I rolled my eyes at her, and she came over and picked up the other arm of the easy chair I was holding. The last thing we needed in this house was another back injury. "Nora will run us into the ground," she said. "We'll be spending all our time cutting up limes for her Pellegrino."

We lugged the stuffed chair backward toward the window. "Don't you have any sympathy for her? After all, she has a real problem. It's like she's trying to hold in triplets with a piece of Scotch tape." Far be it from me to make a case for Nora moving in.

"Triplets!" Sandy cried. "Nobody said anything to me about triplets!" She dropped her side of the chair, and so I dropped mine in sympathy.

"I'm sorry. That really is a shocker. I only just found that part out myself."

While Sandy wept in the easy chair, the two men came back with the mattress and used X-Acto knives to strip off the endless yards of extra heavy plastic wrap before hoisting it onto the frame. They were big men with thick, bulging arms, and still they leaned against the bed and panted for a minute when it was done. The bed was exactly in the center of the room. No concessions were made for trying to work it into the decor.

The shorter of the two men held out a clipboard and a pen. "Sign," he said.

"Don't feel too bad," the big one told Sandy. "My brother's wife had triplets, and they all turned out just fine. They're just like any other kids, only there're three of them."

Sandy didn't look up or stop crying, and so I thanked him for the tip and handed back the clipboard. I asked them to take the plastic wrap with them, but they said they didn't do that.

I looked at Sandy and then at my watch. There wasn't time for everything. I trudged up to get some sheets and pillows and blankets, and Sandy came along behind me, airing her complaints.

"Why does she get everything?" she said.

"Meaning what, exactly? That you wish you had triplets?"

"No, of course not. It's just the abundance of it all. She has to do everything bigger and better than everyone else. It wouldn't be possible for Nora to just have one baby."

"Did everything go okay?" Romeo called out from his room.

"Oh, it's great," I yelled back, looking to see if there was an extra mattress pad somewhere.

"Sorry I couldn't help," he said.

"Very funny."

"The thing is," Sandy said, trying to sound a little bit more rational, "with all respect to you, it's hard to live at home with your mother. It's hard not to fall into those old roles that you had growing up."

"Tell me about it," I said. The pink sheets were old, and all the flowers had faded off, but they were the softest. I noticed that Sandy had that hurt look on her face again. "All I mean is that the things that are hard for you are probably the same things that are hard for me."

"Julie?" Romeo said.

"Yes, love?"

"If you could bring a ginger ale up, I'd really appreciate it. No hurry at all, just the next time you're coming."

"You've got it."

"Okay," Sandy said, "so it's hard for you, too. I accept that. But we've come a long way. We respect each other. We have a good dynamic. I feel like with Nora here . . ."

"You're going to be twelve again and she'll be sixteen and never letting you in her room."

Sandy cocked her head to the side. "Something like that."

I took the bedding down and the ginger ale up. I brought the lunch plates down and the read newspaper down and the bendy straws (which I had forgotten) up. Sandy followed me like a tail follows a dog, talking and talking about the family dynamics she had endured as a teenager and how she wasn't interested in enduring them again in her thirties.

"Don't you need to go to work?" I said, as she helped me pull the top sheet tight over the hospital bed.

"I do. I know I do."

But what did it matter? Five minutes later the doorbell rang, and there stood Alex holding Nora in his arms like a bride.

"This is the new preferred mode of transportation," Nora said.

"I'm good for another ten pounds, tops," Alex said. The way he bounced her up in his arms gave me a little shiver.

"Put her down, Alex. I don't want you hurting yourself."

"I'm not that much of a cow yet," Nora said.

"You are, actually," Alex said.

"Hi, Nora," Sandy said, trying to make an effort. "Hi, Alex."

Alex set his wife on the bed, and she stretched out flat with her arms above her head. On her back, it was clear to see what she had been hiding. There was a significant amount of baby under that baggy shirt, a lot more than what I thought of as nearly four months' worth.

"It seems a little weird to have this right in the middle of the room," she said.

"The guys who brought it over didn't do placement, just delivery."

Alex left to go get the bags, while Nora gave a couple of bounces on the bed. "It's pretty comfortable. Did you try it out?"

"There wasn't time," Sandy said.

Nora looked from me to Sandy and back to me. "So what do we do now?"

"I don't know," I said. "Read a book, watch television. Romeo has some books on tape." I wondered if Nora would be interested in Saint Augustine.

"I thought we could talk, spend some time together," Nora said brightly. Alex came in and set two large suitcases down on the floor, then he left again. "What time do the kids come home?"

"Not until three-thirty," Sandy said. "And Nora, no more lottery tickets. Sarah was crushed that somebody else won the pot."

"There's always another pot."

"But I'm telling you, really, no more."

"Look, I'm in bed. If Mom doesn't sell lottery tickets in the house, I guess I'm not buying them."

"I should get to work," Sandy said.

"Do you have to go in today? It's my first day of bed rest. Can't we have some fun?"

"In bed?" Sandy said.

"Well, it would be awfully boring just to lie here."

She was not quite four months pregnant. No one carried to term with triplets, but still that could be three months, even four months, of awfully boring days.

"I thought that's what bed rest was all about," Sandy said.

Alex came back in the door carrying two more bags.

"Where are you going to put all of this?" Sandy said.

"There are still closets here, aren't there? There's the closet in my old room."

"Sarah lives in your old room," Sandy said. There was an edge to her voice, but she caught it and held up her watch. "Look at this. Boy, am I late."

"You're not late," Nora said. "You know the boss."

"Late, late, late," she said, and ran straight into Alex, who was coming back in with a collection of variously sized tote bags and computer cases. She apologized, waved, and was gone.

Nora looked around the room, taking it all in again from the vantage point of her newly installed bed. "I'm awfully hungry." She smiled at me very nicely. "Could you make me a cheese sandwich?"

"I could," I said, but for some reason the very thought of it made me nervous. I turned and started for the kitchen.

"Mom?"

I turned. I waited.

"It is hormone-free cheese, isn't it?"

"I don't think so," I said. "I don't know why it would be."

"I just assumed, with the children and all, that you'd be feeding them . . ." She stopped and looked at me again. "Why don't you get me a pad of paper and a pen, and I'll make out a shopping list. There are a lot of things I can't eat anymore. In fact, you might just want to read *What to Eat When You're Expecting*. That could be a lot quicker."

"But I probably won't finish it before I go to the grocery."

Alex beamed, so proud of his wife for putting the needs of their little trio first. "I need to get back to the office," he said, and he kissed her.

I don't know why I thought he was going to say, "Let me go to the grocery store for you." It was wrong of me to hope, but I did.

"I hate that he has all this pressure on him," Nora said after he had gone.

"He can handle it," I said.

She tore off the piece of paper and handed it to me. "Let me just have half a cheese sandwich for now. I'll have a little bit of bad food to tide me over until you get back. And Mom?"

"Hmm?"

"Could you take that plastic out of here? I can smell it. It's making me feel a little nauseated."

I sniffed, but I wasn't pregnant and couldn't smell plastic. I dragged the enormous, twisted pile of clear sheeting backward with me into the kitchen, where I kicked it down the back steps, making a mental note to do something about it later. Then I made my pregnant daughter a very bad cheese sandwich. I noticed a peculiar little trembling in my hand as I spread the mustard on the bread. I was her mother, and I knew she liked mustard. I folded it over and put it on a plate and took it out to her with a napkin.

"The bed's not plugged in," she said, fiddling with the control box that stuck up from the side on its metal arm.

"I'll get to that," I said. "I'll need to get an extension cord."

She looked at the sandwich and then she looked at me. "Pellegrino?"

And suddenly the trembling was stronger. My left hand started flopping like a fish against my hip, and I quickly stuck it in my pocket. "I'm out," I said hoarsely. "Do you want a glass of water?"

Nora narrowed her eyes at me, or at least I thought she narrowed her eyes: Maybe I was wrong. "Tap?"

"Yes."

"No."

"Okay."

"But you'll put Pellegrino on the list, and some Evian, too. And limes. I'll need some limes, but make sure they're organic."

I nodded as I was backing away from her. She was asking a question about the remote for the TV, but I was already running up the stairs to tell Romeo I was leaving. I could feel my heart going a million miles a minute in my chest. I stumbled into the room, panting like a coyote in August.

"Did you run up the stairs?" he said, looking concerned.

I nodded too vigorously. "It's good exercise. Nora's here. I'm going to go and get her some things she needs at the store. Do you want anything at the store?" I tried to quell the caged-animal quality in my tone.

He thought for a minute, then he nodded at the ceiling. "I'd like some of those little prethreaded floss picks. I don't know what they're called. I think they have them at CVS. Would you mind?"

"Not a problem," I said. All the air was going out of the room.

"Hey, Julie," Romeo said.

I turned around and gave him a bright smile.

"Slow down a little. You don't need to kill yourself."

I hadn't even thought about it until he mentioned it.

My left hand was still shaking badly, so I drove with my right. I kept telling myself to stay calm, drive slowly, don't make any mistakes, but everything in me wanted to smash down on the accelerator and jump over the curbs, plow through flower beds and trash cans. I was Popeye Doyle and this was *The French Connection*. I had to get out of there. It had only been twenty minutes, and no one had been unpleasant, and I had to get out of there.

I could tell my luck was changing. I hit three green lights in a row, then turned down the alley that took me to the back entrance of Roseman's. I got out of the car and slipped in the back door, praying that no one would see me. I could hear Sandy in the front of the store, talking to a customer, and I slipped right up to the huge metal door and opened it without a sound. I went into the cooler and sealed myself in.

Oh, how I love you, cement floors of my youth! How I love you, white plastic buckets. How I love you, endless rolls of cheap roses from Argentina in every conceivable color and tiny pink carnations that really do smell better than anything and huge, dramatic mums and cheerful flat-faced Gerber daisies hanging in cardboard racks—I love you all, even the indestructible leather leaf fern, and the trembling mists of baby's breath gathered in the corner. I love you, cold air and the sweet smell of living things, and oh, oh, how I love you, cooler, in all your perfectly boxed silence and solitude. All I had needed was the chance to be alone in the place that I knew better than anyplace else in the world.

All of the trembling went up from my hand and through my chest and into my throat, where it released itself in great, gulping sobs. I sat down on an overturned bucket and cried me a river, not even bothering to cover my face with my hands. I knew from experience that a person could make a lot of noise in a cooler and never be heard. I don't know how long I would have gone on, if I hadn't finally felt the light pressure on my knee, a small, warm hand pressing against my leg, then the quiet repetition of my name.

"Julie? Julie?"

I closed my mouth and opened my eyes. Through a blur of tears, I made out the outline of a beautiful girl. It was Audrey Hepburn kneeling right in front of me.

"Hey, honey," she said when I looked at her.

"Hey, Plummy," I said, and hiccupped. "Welcome home."

Chapter Nine

PLUMMY HAD ON A PAIR OF BLUE JEANS WITH THE hem turned up to her knee and an ancient corduroy shirt that I wear sometimes when I'm working in the back. It had been Mort's shirt, and he loved it, but after he ran off with Lila he never had the nerve to come by the shop and take it back. I thought of that shirt as my divorce settlement. Plummy's hair was long and heavy and dark, and she had twisted it up and run the twist through with several of those green sticks we used to hold message cards in bouquets. So how did she manage to look like she had just stepped off the runway at Prada?

"Can I get you anything?" she said kindly over my weeping. "A glass of water? A cup of coffee?"

I shook my head, sending tears in every direction. "I'm sorry."

Plummy reached into her back pocket and pulled out a handkerchief, clean and pressed and embroidered with tiny purple lilacs at each corner. It was completely a gesture from the movies. I couldn't bear the thought of blowing my nose on it.

"Go ahead," she said.

"I never," I said, fighting back a sob. "It's just—"

She smiled at me, and in that smile it was easy to see that for all her success and sophistication she was still a young girl, a very sweet young girl. I tried to focus on the sweetness as a way of calming myself down.

"I cry in the cooler all the time," she said. "As far as I'm concerned that's why they installed them in flower shops in the first place. When I was growing up I always went into the cooler to cry, unless I was going into the cooler to make out with some guy. They're good for that, too. When you've got five brothers and an overprotective father, you learn how to take your privacy where you can."

"I can see that."

"Wait right here." She got up and pulled open the heavy metal door while I took a few deep breaths and tried to reassemble the woman I used to be. I was too tired and too upset even to think about being embarrassed. I'd been caught doing more serious things than crying in a cooler.

Plummy came back holding a tall glass in one hand. "Drink this anyway. You lose all that fluid when you cry."

I sipped the water, and somehow it made me feel calmer. Maybe it was just the fact that someone had brought it to me, instead of me bringing it to someone.

"So I have to ask you, but you don't have to tell me, does this have to do with my father?"

"Oh no," I said, but then I remembered the floss picks. "Well, not in the way you would think. He's getting better, and I love having him around." I looked at her big dark eyes and was struck by how much they reminded me of Romeo's.

"But it's got to be hard."

"It was maybe a little easier when he could stand up."

"And Sandy told me about Nora and the triplets."

I smiled and took another sip. "So you're completely up to date. I don't have to tell you anything at all."

"Triplets." Plummy shook her pretty head. "I still don't think I'm up to taking care of a cat."

"Good," I said. "You stick with that feeling."

The door opened up a little bit, and Sandy said, "Plummy, are you talking to somebody?" then she said, "Mom?"

"I was crying in the cooler," I said.

Sandy sighed. "I've already cried all over Plummy this morning. At least I got her while she was still fresh."

Plummy laughed and pulled another handkerchief out of another pocket to dab her own eyes. I guess she bought them in bulk. "I'm like a duck. It all rolls right off me."

I wiped my face again and finished the water. "I think I really just want to come back to work. I miss this place. Sandy, maybe you should stay home for awhile and run the house and I'll come in."

"In your dreams," Sandy said.

"It's a beautiful store," Plummy said. "Not to be disloyal, but I think it has much better light than Dad's store."

"That's very sweet of you," I said.

Sandy leaned against the door. She seemed like a different person now that she was out of the house. "I just got a call from the school, and they told me that Sarah threw up and wants to come home."

"Too much Halloween candy?"

"It could be, or maybe she worked herself up into a state over this lottery business. Who knows, she might even have the flu, but I need to go get her."

I stood up from my bucket, which was very low, and that, combined with the cold, had left me stiff. "I'll go get her. If she feels like it, I'll take her to the grocery store with me, and we can buy pesticide-free, antibiotic-free, hormone-free saltines for Nora."

"I liked her better when she was just worrying about calories," Sandy said. "Are you sure you don't mind getting Sarah?"

"It will give me a chance to stall for a little while: Besides, I want to spend some time with her. I know she's pretty depressed."

"What's Sarah depressed about?" Plummy asked.

"She didn't win 234 million dollars in the lottery," Sandy said.

Plummy nodded gravely. "I didn't either. I was really down about that, too."

"If I ever see another Mega Millions ticket in our house, you mark my words, there will be hell to pay," Sandy said.

The three of us left the cooler rubbing our arms and stamping our feet. I was all ready to go, but when I was walking past the work bench, I saw the most amazing thing: a bunch of flowers nestled in a low box, ready to go out for delivery. Now, I see flowers all the time, I see them with a professional eye, and nothing knocks the breath out of me anymore—but this did. This was a swirl, a storm of yellow butterflies suspended over a mossy field, tiny yellow orchids on stripped stems, each suspended at a slightly different height, and yet all of them moving together. It was so elegant, so whimsical, so true, that I expected the whole thing to lift up and fly out of the store. I held up my hand to touch and then, instead, I leaned forward and blew.

Plummy clapped her hands. "That's exactly right!" she said. "It should inspire you to move the air around it."

"She's a genius," Sandy said, speaking of Plummy. "I didn't even know there was such a thing as a genius florist until she showed up for work this morning."

Plummy blushed and shook her head. "My dad's pretty good, but he didn't have a lot of room for self-expression. His parents were both squashers."

"My parents weren't squashers, and I never came up with anything close to that," Sandy said. I leaned past her and blew again ever so lightly on the yellow blossoms and made them shiver.

I don't know what exactly had made me feel better—the cry or the talk or the sight of those yellow butterflies. Maybe it was everything. "Good-bye, beautiful girls," I said, and kissed them both. "Thank you."

I left the store feeling thirty pounds and thirty years lighter. I had gone to the very bottom of my sadness and was filled up again with beauty and goodwill. It was a much-needed exchange.

୧୨

The principal of the grade school herself led me back to the nurse's office, where Sarah lay stretched out on a cot with a wet rag over her eyes. I had come to claim my own sickly children from this very office in the past and very likely from this same cot. Always, the sight of them lying there pale and supine broke my heart. That was back in the days when there was a genuine nurse sitting at the desk and not just the office secretary. She glanced up at me from her paperwork and smiled. "I'm Mrs. Oates," she said. "Someone's sick." That was the full extent of her diagnostic capabilities.

"Hello, Button," I said to Sarah.

Sarah lifted one edge of the washrag to look at me. Then she bent her fingers up and down in a weak attempt at a wave.

"Feeling crummy?"

Her head moved against its little paper-covered pillow in half a nod.

The faux nurse checked the paperwork to see that I was in fact registered to claim my granddaughter and not just someone who trolled nurses' offices looking to collect sick children. I signed a release form and peeled Sarah off the tiny bed.

She was wilted. Everything about her seemed damp and limp as a jonquil beaten flat by a violent rain. I held her hand as she wobbled down the hallway and out the door without so much as a word; but as soon as we stepped outside, and that bright November wind smacked her in the face, she seemed to perk up immeasurably. She took a long, deep breath and then got into the car.

I noticed the sudden resurgence of color in her cheeks. "How are you now?" I asked.

She sniffed and touched her fingers to her forehead. "If I say I feel better, do I have to go back?"

"No."

"I think I feel better."

I leaned over and kissed the part of her hair. "Good."

"Do you ever just feel like you need to get out of a place?"

"As a matter of fact, yes. Was something going on at school?"

She leaned her head back against the seat and closed her eyes. "The other kids were teasing me about not winning the lottery."

"Why? I'm assuming they didn't win, either."

"They never said they were going to win."

"I see." I backed out of the parking lot, crunching through the last of the fall leaves. "Do you feel well enough to go to the grocery store with me, or do I need to take you home?"

"Will you buy me a lottery ticket?"

I put the car in park and turned around to get a good look at her. "Listen, Sarah, this has got to end. Your mother says so, I say so. It isn't good for you. Eight-year-olds aren't supposed to gamble. We never should have started letting you play in the first place. Life doesn't work like a movie. You're not Charlie, and there is no golden ticket. It's a wonderful thing to imagine, but it's also a wonderful thing to live in the real world, okay? We all want you to live in the real world with us."

Sarah looked down at her lap. She gave the shoulder strap on her seat belt a couple of distracted tugs. "I'm supposed to win," she said quietly.

I folded my hands over the top of the steering wheel and tried to think of a way to explain this that wouldn't crush every ounce of joy out of life. "No, you're not, darling, no more or less than anybody else. When those numbers come up they don't come up for you or against you, they just come up."

"We could do a lot with that money," she said.

"You're absolutely right, and so could everybody else, too. You don't want to spend your life with your head in the clouds, wanting things you don't have. We've got a very nice life just the way we are."

"I think I'm feeling sick again."

I patted her knee. I felt for the kid, I really did. It was neither greed nor entitlement that she suffered from. She had simply believed in the fairy tale, just like any other kid who thought that little pigs built their houses in defense of huffing wolves. "Okay, I'll take you home."

She shook her head. "No, let's go to the grocery store. I'm just tired, is all. I'm not going to throw up or anything."

Even in the health food grocery store, there were still plenty of cookies and ginger ale and Gummy bears and magazines to be had, all the sorts of things that grandmothers were perfectly willing to buy sick granddaughters who had recently lost their betting privileges. And Sarah wasn't pushing her luck. All she asked for was a demure box of whole-wheat animal crackers.

We had a long list, and neither of us was in such a hurry to get home again, so we coasted slowly through the wide aisles of Bread & Circus, where I thought I'd have better luck finding the eggs of chickens who had taken free range of the south of France. When we rounded the corner to contemplate a collection of organic soups, my cart was rammed head-on by my friend Gloria.

"You never shop here!" she said.

"It's too expensive," I said. "These eggs are five dollars a dozen." I picked up the eggs and peered inside the carton to make sure that none of them had been broken on impact.

"And aren't you supposed to be in school?" Gloria said to Sarah. "They still have school, don't they?"

"I'm sick," Sarah said. "I was sick."

Gloria immediately put a hand on Sarah's forehead as if to test the validity of her statement. "You're not hot, but you're pale. Will they let you out of school for being pale?"

"They will if you throw up on them," Sarah said sensibly.

Gloria had abandoned her own cart and was now sorting through mine. "Japanese seaweed crackers, tofu, baby eggplants, raw goat cheese. No wonder this child is feeling punk."

"It's not for Sarah, it's for Nora."

"Since when do you do Nora's grocery shopping?"

"She's going to have three babies," Sarah said.

It's amazing how quickly we adapt to news. I had known about Nora's pregnancy for such a short period of time, and already I could hear the words without my mouth going dry. But when I saw the news hitting Gloria like a fast right hook, I was reminded that this was indeed still a shocking thing.

She wrapped her fingers through the slender metal bars of my basket and blinked. "Nora doesn't like children."

"She likes me," Sarah said.

"But what are the chances she'd get three like you?" Gloria stumbled on the word three. It was hard for her even to say it.

"I don't know," Sarah said, obviously pleased at the thought of three little versions of herself. "She's my aunt. I guess it could happen."

"Oh, Julie," Gloria said. "How could you not have told me?" Her eyes were bright and glazed in tears. For Gloria, who told me everything and was used to hearing everything, this was a genuine betrayal.

"I've only known since last night, and in case you've forgotten, I've had my hands full over at my house. I was going to call you as soon as I had two minutes in a row."

"You can call me at three o'clock in the morning."

"But wait," I said. "The story gets better."

"Four babies?" Sarah said.

A skinny woman in a navy warm-up suit who was pushing her cart past us slowed down at that and turned to look at me. Massachusetts is not by its nature a particularly nosy place, but any thinking woman would have to stop at the mention of a quartet delivery. I shook my head no, and she sailed off down the aisle looking relieved.

"She has an incompetent cervix, and she's on total bed rest."

"That's awful!" Gloria said. "So you have to do all her shopping?"

"She's on total bed rest in a hospital bed that is *in my living room*."

"Nora's living in the living room?" Sarah asked excitedly. All of the real action had transpired during her brief appearance in school, probably furthering her belief that she was better off staying home.

While Sarah's joy at having another captive audience member was evident, Gloria said nothing. She only blinked. Since the death of my parents, Gloria was the person who had known me better and longer than anyone else in the world. She was the maid of honor at my wedding and came with me to the lawyer for my divorce. We have taken care of each other's kids and borrowed each other's clothes and attended each other's hysterectomies. We have, for richer and for poorer, for better and for worse, in sickness and in health, stuck by each other. So I cannot say it surprised me when Gloria just sat down on the floor of the very clean Bread & Circus, rested her back gently against a display of soup cans, put her face in her hands, and started to cry.

"Hey," Sarah said, touching Gloria's shoulder. "It's okay. Nora's going to be okay. She might even want to name one of the babies after you."

"Baby Gloria," I said, and took my place beside her on the floor and held her knee. Sarah sat down as well, impressed to see adults behaving so far outside the range of normal behavior.

Gloria laughed a little bit into her hands. "You're completely doomed," she said. "You know that, right?"

"I do."

"Romeo upstairs, Nora downstairs, everybody else running around."

"Don't forget about the visitors," I said.

"They come every two minutes," Sarah said. "Especially the priest and his brother."

Gloria shook her head. "What are you going to do with three babies?"

"Ah!" I held up my hand. "Correction: What is *Nora* going to do with three babies?"

"Forgive me. You know what I mean."

"We just haven't gotten that far. For now, we only have to concern ourselves with hatching them." I looked at my watch, suddenly remembering that I'd left a houseful of defenseless invalids alone too long. A pretty young girl rolled past us with a baby propped up in the front of her cart. She pointed us out to the baby and told her to wave, but the baby only blinked and blew a little bubble of spit.

"This is where you get them," Gloria whispered to Sarah. "Over on aisle five. Why does anyone go through all the trouble of making them at home when you can just throw one in the cart?"

Sarah giggled at such talk.

"Okay, girls, enough of this foolishness. I have an infirmary to run."

We hoisted each other up off the floor and resumed our shopping. Gloria, who was a much more enlightened eater than I have ever been, gave me some guidance as to what Nora would find acceptable. Then we steered our carts into the checkout line, me behind Gloria.

"Have you won the lottery yet?" Gloria asked Sarah, as the last of her groceries were tucked into their bags.

Far above Sarah's head I mouthed the word, "No."

"Not yet," Sarah said sadly.

"Well, don't give up. You just have to keep trying. It's all about beating the odds, you know. You can't win if you don't play."

"I know," Sarah said.

Gloria kissed us both and promised to come over soon to visit everyone. She said she was anxious to see if Nora looked fat. "Courage!" she said as she wheeled away. I thought she was saying it to me and Sarah thought she was saying it to her and we both gave weak, sad smiles in return.

I pushed the cart up to the checkout and made myself busy unloading the pricey whole-grain items onto the black conveyer belt. I didn't want to look at Sarah, and I didn't want to look at the bright Massachusetts State Lottery sign that told us that playing would be fun. Sarah always wanted to ride along to the grocery store with me, and for the first time, I realized it wasn't because the grocery store was such a great time for her. It was because I always bought her a ticket. If there was a problem, it was as much my responsibility as anyone else's. Sarah stood on her toes to reach down into the basket and hand me the lemon hummus and the plain fat-free yogurt and the very first clementines of the season.

"Do you think Gloria doesn't want Aunt Nora to have babies?" she asked me.

I shook my head with as much reassurance as I could muster. "It's nothing like that. It's just that she's worried. She knows it's going to be a lot of work."

"But we can do it," Sarah said. "If we all work at it together. Mom and I can watch one of the babies and you and Romeo can watch one and Aunt Nora and Uncle Alex can watch one. It's not too many when you think about it that way." She handed me a bag of limes and some all-natural Parmesan bread sticks that actually looked pretty good.

"No, it's not so bad."

A thin young boy who should have been in school himself loaded the bags back in the basket for me, and we pushed them off toward the electric door and the cold bright day outside. Sarah was walking as slowly as was humanly possible, and I slowed down further and further to stay beside her. And then I did something I cannot explain. I turned the cart around and marched right up to the information desk.

"I want to buy a lottery ticket," I said.

"How many?" The woman behind the counter was writing out some numbers on a piece of paper. She did not look up at me.

"Just one." I turned around and looked at Sarah, and she was beaming. Light was practically radiating from her head.

"Just one," I said to her. "Do you understand me? One last ticket, and you don't tell anyone. After this, it's over. I won't break down again, okay? This one ticket, then we turn the whole thing off for good."

"Okay." She wrapped her arms around my waist and buried her face in my stomach, squeezing me with all of the love she contained. I knew that what I was doing was wrong, but it had been a long day, and a single dollar had given both of us a much-needed bounce toward joy.

"What do you want?" the woman said.

"Mass Millions," I told her. "Quick pick."

Sarah looked up at me with a puzzled expression.

"It's time for a change," I said, remembering that Sandy had declared a Fatwa against the Mega Millions.

When we were in the car, Sarah put the ticket in her shoe. "This is all I needed," she said, and pulled her laces snug again. "Thank you, thank you, thank you."

"And you're never going to tell."

"I'm never going to tell," she said. "Unless it's the winning ticket. If it is the winning ticket, then I'm going to want to tell Mommy."

"I think that's fair."

We stopped off at CVS and picked up the prethreaded floss picks for Romeo, and while we were at it, we got three packs of baseball bubble gum cards for Little Tony and a box of Hot Tamales for Big Tony and a bottle of Whisper Pink nail polish that Sarah picked out for her mother. After that, we drove home in glory. We had every last thing that everybody wanted. We were rich.

Chapter Ten

For the first few days of Nora's bed rest, every time Alex came to visit, he lugged in another box of things that she simply could not do without. He brought over a very practical little desk on wheels that looked exactly like those things that nurses put hospital trays on to conveniently suspend them over the bed, except this one was made out of cherrywood or teak and Nora quickly covered it with papers from the various boxes. She sat with the bed positioned upright, a headset plugged into her cell phone, her laptop computer plugged into the wall, and continued to run her empire from my living room in Somerville.

"The property in north Cambridge is perfect for them," she was saying as I tried to the best of my ability to pass unnoticed up the stairs, but Nora never missed me. She started snapping. Snap, snap, snap. I took a deep breath and turned to face her.

She was pointing to a file box on the floor. Snap and point, snap, snap, point. I pointed to myself, then to the box, and she nodded with enormous exasperation.

"One minute," she said. "My girl is bringing me the file now." She covered the speaking wand with her hand and said, a bit too sharply, "Jackson!"

Now really, if she could cover the mouthpiece to say Jackson, couldn't she cover it long enough to say, "Mother, could you hand me the Jackson file in that box?" It wasn't as if I was looking for "please." But she had already thrown up twice this morning and I knew this was trying for her as well, so I picked up the file and handed it to her. She did not look up.

"I know they want four bathrooms, but that's what closets are for. The downstairs closet is absolutely begging to become a half bath. There's the answer."

If Sarah and Little Tony weren't so thoughtlessly engaged in their elementary education during the day, they would have been the ones doing the fetching. Both children, it seemed, longed for nothing in this world but to be personal assistants, and they were training at the elbow of the master CEO.

Nora demanded that they do their homework the same way she demanded they bring her another cup of herbal tea, check the printer cable, and fold, stamp, and seal all documents before taking them out to the mailbox. She checked their spelling and math problems between calls. She let them type up the poems they wrote for English class on her computer while sitting beside her in the bed, each waiting for the other to complete his or her turn. She let Tony play Hangman on her Palm Pilot while she let Sarah watch her daily dose of *Wonka,* and if Sarah wished that she had the Palm and Tony wanted to put on a different movie, neither of them made a peep about it. Nora did not tolerate one word of bickering. Bickering in any form got on her nerves and resulted in the immediate banishment of both parties from the living room, no matter who had instigated said bickering. Nora ran a very tight ship.

I suppose I should have admired her, the way she never stopped. But Nora's industriousness and decisiveness made Sandy and me feel like a couple of blind moles searching our way through pudding. It was frankly impossible for me to believe that Nora's cervix, or any other part of Nora's being, was incompetent. The tornados she spun out from the stillness of her bed only made me tired.

In a way, I was coming to understand my formerly ill-behaved, formerly teenaged daughter: She just had too much energy. Even back then, she had wanted to rule the world. Until she found real estate as a means of channeling her powers, she was simply too much to bear.

She snapped at me again, and my eyes came back into focus.

I had simply been standing there. She handed me the Jackson file, still talking a million miles a minute.

"Do they really think that Greenspan is going to keep the interest rates at Nixon administration levels much longer? The time to move is now!"

Then she snapped and pointed to the box where the file should be returned. Had she been a child, I would have whacked her over the head with the file—not hard enough actually to hurt her, but hard enough to startle her into a clear realization of what it meant to snap at one's mother. But she was pregnant, and it wasn't good to whack one's pregnant daughter, even with a paper file, no matter how badly one wanted to.

I carefully put the file back into its correct slot and looked again to Nora, but she only pointed to the phone. The phone that she perhaps thought I hadn't noticed before. She wanted to tell me that she was very busy, and I should go.

I do not remember my mother ever assuming the role of handmaid in my life, not even for an instant. That is not to say that she didn't take care of me and my brother. The food was good and the house was clean and the budget was sufficiently tight and fair so that we always had enough but never too much.

But my mother and father lived in what I thought of as the adult world while my brother and I lived in the children's world, and while those two planets could peacefully coexist, they had a very specific order of gravity. The children revolved around the parents, never the other way around. When I was nine years old, I could no more imagine my mother sitting on the floor with us to play a game of Monopoly than I could imagine getting out of bed to join one of their cocktail parties and being greeted with a cigarette and a Manhattan. I was there to set the table and hang out the laundry and do whatever little things my mother was too busy to attend to. I was a child, and my duty was to be of service to the world of adults. My brother used to say my parents had children because they didn't want to have to pay anybody to work in the shop. No one ever questioned that or even felt bad about it, that's just the way life was.

Even when I was a grown woman with children of my own, I still felt that I was somehow less than adult when in the presence of my very adult mother. Had I been smart, I would have realized that one can only truly feel like an adult in relationship to one's own children.

But I wasn't smart. I was a tenderhearted sap who wanted to be close to my girls and make sure they never suffered a moment's alienation. So instead of marching them off to their room at the first sign of bad behavior, I learned to use the hula hoop. I let them stay up late on weekends and fall asleep in our bed watching movies. I gave them my lipstick and attended all of their basketball games and gave them every opportunity to be open and honest with their accessible mom, and what happened? They still managed to seal themselves off on another planet. The difference was that their planet did not revolve around mine.

Long after I had completely lost control of the situation, it occurred to me that my mother had been right after all. If you spend too much time trying to be somebody's pal, you'll only wind up getting snapped at down the line.

I went upstairs to check on Romeo, dreaming of the days when I had nothing to do but strip thorns off roses for hours at a time.

My handsome fellow was sitting up in a chair reading a magazine. He was wearing jeans and a polo shirt. He was wearing shoes. His hair was wet and neatly parted, and when I walked into the room and gaped at him with frank amazement, he smiled.

"Ta-da!" he said, opening his arms.

"Did you take a shower?"

"I did."

I went over and knelt beside him, resting my hands lightly on his knees. "Romeo, you shouldn't do that. Nobody was upstairs. You could have killed yourself."

"Do I look dead?"

"Actually, you look very clean."

"I'm really getting better. I'm going to go down those stairs tonight."

"No." I felt a great, unaccountable sob rise up in my throat. He couldn't leave me here alone like this. "You're not ready."

"I think I might be ready. I'm feeling good. Do you know what I've been thinking about all morning?"

You've been thinking about not leaving me. You've been thinking about the fact that you never want to spend another night away from me again. "What?"

"I'm going to paint your ceiling."

"No," I said weakly. "No."

"Seriously, you have some water stains. They're faint, but I've had plenty of time to think about them. I don't want you to think I'm sticking my nose in where it doesn't belong, but I really think we should paint the whole room. Find a new color, lighten the place up."

"The water stains are old. Ten years old. There was a little leak and I had to put a new roof on and there just wasn't the money to paint. To tell you the truth, I just got used to them." My voice cracked a little at the end of the sentence.

Romeo put his hand on my head. "Are you upset about the paint? We don't have to paint. It's a great room. The color is fine."

"No, I'm just a little tired, that's all. We can paint it someday."

"But that's how I know I'm really better. I feel like painting it now. I've been very focused on this."

"Well, not tonight, okay?"

"Not tonight." He touched my cheek. "How's Nora?"

"She's taking me down to a pulp," I said.

He scooted over in his chair. "Come here." He patted the tiny sliver of fabric beside him, a sliver that represented approximately one-eighth of the space I would comfortably need to wedge myself into that chair.

"Romeo."

"Come here," he said, and his voice was dreamy and low, and I just fell into it.

I was a woman who needed to be held, a woman who needed to be kissed. I was sick and tired of playing nurse without having any opportunity to play doctor. I pulled my stiffening knees out of the lock position. I straightened up, balanced precariously on the arm of the chair, and leaned over. I was very careful to come at him straight on. "Hold still," I whispered. I kissed him with sincerity and lust.

We were still very much in the game. We hadn't been on the bench so long that we'd lost our confidence. Romeo slipped a hand beneath my sweater, kissing, kissing while his fingers tapped up my ribs and lightly touched the underwire of my bra. That was the moment, that was the hopeful place we were at, when the door swung open.

Who knows what combination of factors come together to create an accident? Was it the kiss, the door, the slender arm of the chair? Was it simply the surprise of three startled adults that sent me straight back, hitting the floor first with my shoulder, then my head?

The sound of the crack alone would have been enough to make me faint, and for an instant I did go out, either from pain or disappointment or simple exhaustion. I closed my eyes and gave myself over to the darkness studded with stars. My feet stayed straight up in the air and rested on the chair arm where once I sat.

"Dad! Don't get up!" I heard a voice say from very far away. "Are you okay? Are you hurt?"

Had Romeo fallen as well? Had the whole chair tipped back? I tried to find words from deep in the recesses of my mind. I wanted to comfort this stranger in my darkness, to tell him, no, I'm fine. Don't worry about me.

But I didn't have to. Romeo answered instead. "No," he said, "I'm okay. Julie? Are you okay?"

Did they notice I was suddenly missing? Did they hear the explosion that was my head hitting the wood floor?

"Julie?"

Someone lowered my legs onto the floor and straightened me out. Should they move me? Was that right?

"That was a fall, all right," Big Tony said. "Open up."

I opened my eyes and looked at him. Where was the panic, the concern?

"You really got the wind knocked out of you. Do you want to stand up?"

"Julie?" Romeo said. "Are you okay down there?"

"Dad, really, she's fine. Don't get up. You're going to hurt your back again."

"Sure," I said, "I'm fine. Just give me a second."

I saw Big Tony's feet walk away, and a minute later he was pulling me up to sip a glass of water. It was how the Cacciamanis comforted those in pain.

"Drink it slow," he said, and helped me hold the glass. "You know, I should go to medical school just so I can look after the people in this house. I could go into neurology, obstetrics, orthopedics, pediatrics"—he looked at me and smiled—"trauma."

"That's funny," I said, and handed back the glass. There was a huge pain in my shoulder and a hot throbbing in the back of my head. "I'm just going to stretch out for a second." I was not feeling so great. I just lay back on the floor and felt enormously comforted by its stillness. I closed my eyes.

"Are you sure you're okay?" Romeo said.

"Sure," I said drowsily.

They waited for a minute, gave a single beat of silence in my honor, and dove right into their conversation.

"I'm serious, Dad. I've been thinking it over. I want to go to medical school."

"Well," Romeo said.

"I know it. I'm almost thirty-seven and I don't have any money and I have Sandy and the kids to think about. But what about the future? It's a huge risk, I know, but I'd be making an investment in myself, an investment that I think would pay off for all of us in the long run."

"That's true, but you have to—"

"There's a lot to think about." Tony sighed and stretched out his legs. Tony liked to sit on the floor. I think it must have been all those years he spent in the Peace Corps, then the World Health Organization, working in countries so third-world that they didn't have stools. "For one thing, we'd have to stay here for at least another five years, and that's not what Sandy and I want. No offense to you, Julie, you've been great, but everybody needs their own space."

Everybody but you, Julie, is what he meant. Doesn't anybody ask? Doesn't anybody stop to wonder how I would feel about another five years living like the Ingalls family, all together in the little prairie house?

"What does Sandy think?" Romeo asked.

"She wants me to be happy. She says she wouldn't care if I drove the delivery truck for the rest of my life, and she doesn't care if we have to struggle through medical school. She just wants me to not feel like I've missed my chance in life."

My daughter, I thought, was both wise and kind.

"Then we're with Sandy," Romeo said. "I just wish I had the money to send you."

Tony laughed, and I heard him clap his father on the leg. "Nobody expects their parents to send them through medical school. I just wanted to talk to you about it, so if you thought I was crazy, you'd have the chance to stop me."

"I don't want to stop you," Romeo said.

And then, just in case anyone was looking for a sign from God or a sign from the AMA, Dominic and Father Al walked into the bedroom. Not only did they no longer ring the doorbell, they had ceased to make any sound when coming up the stairs. I suppose I should feel lucky that Tony put the kibosh on our tryst when he did.

"This is an interesting exchange," the doctor said. "One of

you looks considerably better and one of you looks considerably worse."

"Romeo's better, and I'm resting," I said. I had no interest in trying to open my eyes.

"Julie fell off the chair," Romeo said.

"Oh Julie!" said Father Al, and he knelt beside me and took my hand. It was extremely endearing.

"Let's take a look at you," Dominic said.

"She said she was okay," Tony said, as if he might be accused of some sort of negligence on the very day he announced his interest in the profession.

Al and Dominic pulled me up to a seated position and I can honestly say I wish they hadn't. My head was throbbing almost as badly as my shoulder. Dominic dug around in his bag of tricks and pulled out a penlight, which he shined in my eyes just long enough to bother me, then he started hunting around in my hair.

"What?" Tony asked.

"Well, she's got a little cut. There's some blood back here."

"Blood?" Romeo said.

"Not too much. You could get a stitch or two."

He asked Tony for a wet, warm washcloth, a cotton ball, and a bottle of alcohol, all of which would clean things up and give him a better look at the situation. While he cleaned and dabbed, I just kept quiet.

Suddenly I was hoping for a bad report. A night in the hospital, maybe two, would be nearly as good as the Charles Hotel. I would have a button I could push when I needed something, not that I would ever abuse it. I could fluff my own pillows. No, it was really just a matter of peace and quiet, and the lack of stairs.

"No," Dominic said, blowing lightly on the back of my head to take the sting off. "I really don't think it's worth the trouble of stitches. It isn't bad at all. Take a couple of aspirin and put some ice on your shoulder. I think you're going to be fine. I can check on it when I come back tomorrow."

I stood up slowly and swayed a little. I was ready to go.

"Are you *sure* you're okay?" Romeo asked. He was a good man. I knew if the circumstances were different, he would have gone for the ice.

"I'm fine."

"I'd never met Nora before," Dominic said. "That's really something, her having triplets."

"It is indeed."

"What with her on bed rest downstairs and this one on bed rest upstairs, we really couldn't have let you go to the hospital anyway," Dominic said.

I knew that was supposed to be my laugh line, but I didn't laugh. I just left them there, talking about medicine and what Tony's future held.

Ice sounded like a wonderful idea. I was almost to the kitchen when I heard Nora's voice.

"Mother?"

I walked back and looked at her. She was off the phone. She still had her headset on but the wand was pointing down toward her collarbone. "Yes?"

"I think I'm ready to eat something."

"What would that be?"

"There's still some organic chicken salad, right? So I'll have that, wheat bread, toasted, no extra mayonnaise, lettuce, red grapes on the side. Do you have red grapes?"

"Yes."

"Seedless?"

I wanted to ask her if seeded grapes posed a threat to her pregnancy, because otherwise she could just spit the seeds out like the rest of us. But they were, in fact, seedless grapes, so I didn't have to go there. "Yes."

"And a Pellegrino with just a splash of cranberry and a lime."

I started to nod, but it made my head hurt, so I just said okay and went out to the kitchen.

"Mother?"

I went back.

"You're sure you got the organic chicken salad?"

And this time I didn't say anything. I couldn't say anything, unless it was going to be something I would very deeply regret later on. I just looked at her in a way that I hoped said, *Yes, it is organic, now never ask me that question again,* then I went back to the kitchen.

Father Al was there, rifling through my kitchen drawers. "What do you need, Al?"

"I'm sorry," he said. He looked like he'd been caught trying to steal a spoon. "I'm looking for Baggies."

"Under the sink."

"Sit down," he said, and pulled out a chair for me.

"I need to make Nora's lunch."

"I can do that," he said.

"I'm not going to have you waiting on my children," I said.

He took out two Baggies, a big one and a little one, and filled them both with ice. He draped a dish towel on my shoulder and very gently placed the first bag across it like a saddle. Then he wrapped up the second one and handed it to me. "Hold this on the back of your head."

I did that, then I took the aspirin he gave me.

"Now, tell me what she wants to eat or I'll just make it up."

I didn't have the energy to argue and make the meal and hold the ice on my head, so I told him with all the specificity I could remember what Nora wanted on her sandwich. "I really can do this," I said, but oh, the cold was sweet. It bit into me slowly and froze the pain.

"I'm going to tell you a story," Al said, putting the two slices of bread in the toaster. "Can I make one for you, too?"

"I'm really not hungry, but thanks." I was unused to priests offering me food from my own kitchen, but it didn't actually feel like a bad thing.

"So here's the story." He opened the refrigerator and took out the lettuce from the crisper drawer. "A great flood comes along and a very devout man is in his house praying for the Lord's help. The water comes in through the door, and he goes up to the second floor, then he goes up to the roof, all the while praying to God to be saved. Have you heard this one?"

"Honestly, no."

"Good." He ran the lettuce under the tap one leaf at a time, then began to pat it down with paper towels. "After awhile a man with a boat comes, and says, 'The water is still rising. Get in my boat, and I'll take you to safety.' But the man on the roof says, 'No, the Lord will protect me.'" He opened up the refrigerator and starts looking around.

"Third shelf."

Al took the chicken salad out and started again. "It's still raining, and the water's still rising, and after some time there is another boat with several people in it, and they offer a spot to the man on the roof. They beg him to come, but he says, 'No, the Lord will provide for me.' More rain, more water, the man is now balanced on top of his chimney, and a motor raft goes by, and the pilot says, 'I'll throw you a rope! I'll save you!' But again the man on the roof turns down the help. And when the water swells again, he drowns."

"Great story." I readjusted the ice pack on my shoulder. "Thanks."

Al looked at me and shook his head. "But it's not over. The man goes up to heaven and meets Saint Peter at the gate and Saint Peter sends him straight to God, who greets him warmly. And the man from the roof says, 'Lord, I prayed to you. I believed in you, and you didn't save me.' And God says, 'I sent you three boats. What more did you want?'"

With that, Al garnished the plate with grapes and picked up the Pellegrino and went into the living room to serve my daughter lunch.

Chapter Eleven

NORA WASN'T THE ONLY PERSON WHO HAD MOVED into the living room. Though no one exactly mentioned it, Alex was living there, too. He got home very late and he left very early, but if you happened to be up at the right hour, there he was in the kitchen wearing a pair of pajama bottoms, drinking coffee in the dark. I would have thought, with all the people living in this house and all the other people coming and going, that I wouldn't even notice one extra son-in-law. But the first time I ran into him at five o'clock in the morning, the morning after I fell off the chair, I almost screamed.

"Sh!" he whispered. "Nora's still asleep."

"When did you get here?" I pulled the swinging kitchen door shut behind me. I was whispering, though I felt a little stupid doing it. I had woken up too early because my shoulder was still sore, and I had a hard time getting comfortable.

He looked at the clock over the kitchen sink. "About seven hours ago."

"Where do you sleep?"

He pushed his eyebrows together as if he were suddenly worried that what he was doing might be against house rules. "With Nora?"

"In a single bed?"

He shrugged. "She doesn't roll over anymore." He got up and poured me a cup of coffee which I accepted gratefully.

"Have you slept here before?"

He nodded. "I always sleep here."

"And I just haven't seen you?"

"I guess not."

I wracked my brain for some evidence of Alex in my house. Yes, come to think of it, the coffee was made most mornings when I came downstairs, but I'd chalked that up to Big Tony. Usually Alex came by in the evening, but I always thought he left after I went to bed. I couldn't remember seeing so much as an extra shirt or tie around the house. "Where are your things?"

"I keep stuff at the gym, or I just run by the condo and shower."

"Alex, you don't live anywhere near here."

"It's not so bad," he said. "Anyway, Nora thinks we've already taken up as much space over here as we need to."

"Well, you're certainly welcome." But in truth, it was difficult to imagine one more person waiting for the shower or one more extra towel in the wash. I liked Alex, though I never really felt like I knew him. Like Nora, he worked all the time. He was always on the run.

"I appreciate that." He smiled at me, a handsome shirtless man in my kitchen who in the dim light looked no older than a skinny high school boy. "I don't know what I'd do without you, Julie. If Nora had to stay home by herself all day—" He shook his head. "Well, you know Nora. It would be a disaster for her. Nora always has to be around people."

Did she? Maybe I didn't know Nora.

Alex looked at his watch. "I ought to get cracking."

"I'm going to take some coffee up to Romeo," I said.

"How's he doing up there?"

"Oh, he's great. He's going to be downstairs any day now."

"That's great," Alex said. "I'll look forward to seeing him."

Alex was the only person in this traffic jam of family who didn't make himself at home on the second floor, and, frankly, I appreciated it.

The truth was, I really didn't know when Romeo would

come downstairs. Had we kept a chart of his recovery it would have looked like the stock market: he was up, he was down, he was flat. Some days I found him fully dressed and on the landing at the top of the stairs. "I'm ready," he'd say, but then he'd look down those stairs like a man in a barrel peering over Niagara Falls. I once saw him put one foot down, then bring it right back up.

"What if we put Tony on one side and me on the other and we'll just walk you down?"

"That's it!" he said. "That's the perfect idea. We'll do it tomorrow."

But then tomorrow would roll around, and Romeo would be flat out again. Something would have gone funny in the night, and he couldn't even sit up in the morning.

When I brought him his coffee this morning, he was on the phone.

"No, I really thought today was going to be the day." He smiled at me when I walked in the door and blew me a little kiss. "It's crazy. Maybe I've developed some sort of stair-related phobia. It doesn't feel like a phobia. It actually feels like my back, but I don't know. With everybody else who's coming in and out of here, maybe I should hire a psychiatrist to come by, too."

I put the coffee down on the bedside table and waited.

"That's true," he said. "Al has some training in that stuff. He might be able to talk me down. . . . I know, it's crazy that I haven't seen you. But you're all right? You're feeling all right? . . . That's great. . . . No, you don't have to tell me. The service in this place is terrific." At this Romeo winked at me. "That's right. We may just stay in bed forever. Well, you take care of yourself. . . . Yeah, with any luck I'll get to see you soon. Okay. That's right, you too. Take care." Romeo inched himself up enough to get to his coffee. "Great girl," he said.

"Which great girl?"

"That was Nora. She was calling from downstairs."

It never occurred to me that upstairs and downstairs, the two completely separate parts of my existence ever communicated with one another.

"I really need to go downstairs and see her," Romeo said.

"I think you should just relax and stay where you are."

"For how long? You can't spend the rest of your life running up and down the stairs, bringing me coffee and sandwiches."

"I could."

"My mother doesn't even want to talk to me anymore. I call over there on the phone, and she says to Theresa, 'Tell him I'm busy.' I don't think she remembers who I am."

"She's remembered you for sixty-three years. It isn't going to kill her to forget you for a few weeks."

Romeo puzzled on this one for a minute, then came up with

another angle. "And what about work? I have to get back to work."

But work was going suspiciously well. When I managed to grab a minute to run by the stores, they both seemed to be thriving. Word had gotten out that the hottest floral designer in New York had landed temporarily in Somerville, and everyone was changing their events in order to get a spot on her dance card. Because Plummy was a minimalist, we had nearly doubled our sales while ordering almost no extra flowers, except of course for those tiny orchids, which were practically her signature. Fewer flowers, higher volume, and all for more money (she had raised the prices). Sandy was right about Plummy's being a genius.

∞

Plummy had only planned to stay for a week, but when her week was up none of us mentioned it, and she didn't seem so eager to go. One night after work there was a chipper knock on the bedroom door. Plummy and Sandy burst into the room like a couple of giggling junior high school girls. Sandy was carrying an incredibly tall, slender clear vase, a nearly unusable size that we kept around for sending out bunches of sunflowers.

"We brought Daddy some flowers," Plummy said, and then leaned over to kiss her father's forehead. "Hi, Daddy!"

But neither Romeo nor I could say a thing, and when the girls saw us mesmerized by the flowers, they started laughing again. The whole arrangement existed inside the vase. Not a single leaf tip came over the top. The bottom was weighted with round gray stones, and the flowers were all tiny, swirls of pink and lavender with a few bright smears of yellow. It was something you wanted to hold in your hands and turn like a kaleidoscope. There seemed to be no end to the different ways you could consider it.

Romeo sighed, "Plummy, I don't know what to say. This is magnificent."

And then the girls howled. "Not me!" Plummy said. "I didn't do one blossom. Not one thought. It's Sandy's!"

"Sandy?" I said.

"Don't act too shocked, or you'll hurt my feelings," Sandy said, but the smile on her face was huge. "Plummy's been giving me and Raymond some pointers."

"Raymond's a little less open-minded," Plummy said.

"She taught you how to do this?" I said. I couldn't believe it. If this was what she was teaching, then I wanted to go to the class.

"This is all Sandy," Plummy said. "I've only shown her how to take some risks."

"I want to do aquarium-inspired pieces," Sandy said. "I want to put the flowers under glass."

"Then I think you're a genius, too." I got up and gave Sandy a kiss, and she threw her arms around my neck. I could all but feel the energy vibrating out of her curls. She was so excited by what she had done, and I had to wonder when the last time was that Sandy had a second in the spotlight. "I think we have two floral geniuses in the same family."

Soon after that Big Tony came in with Little Tony and Sarah from ice-skating, and they all made a raucous fuss over Sandy's arrangement.

"You've got to bring it to my school," Little Tony said. "I want to show it to my class. You could give a talk about flower arranging."

"She's bringing it to *my* class," Sarah said.

"We sent two of these out today, and both of the people called up and said they wanted to send out three more tomorrow," Plummy said. "Pretty soon we're going to be so busy, we're going to need a third store."

"Hopefully one we can run out of the bedroom," Romeo said.

When the phone rang, I was the one who answered it.

"What's going on up there?" Nora said. "It sounds like you're trying to teach moose how to foxtrot."

"We are," I said. "It turns out they're very graceful."

"Well, somebody should come downstairs. It's a little lonely down here." I looked at the clock and saw that it was past six, just about the time that Nora would be getting off work. There was no one left to bark at on the cell phone after six o'clock, there was only us.

"I'll send down an ambassador. The rest of us will be down in a little bit. We're talking flowers."

I asked Sarah if she'd be a good sport and go visit Aunt Nora, and as quick as a shot she was out of the bedroom and taking the stairs in sets of three.

"One stair at a time," Sandy called after her, but Sarah was already gone. In another minute we heard the opening bars of *Wonka,* that faux-Strauss waltz of pouring chocolate and dancing lollypops. Everybody in the room groaned.

"That's ridiculous," Sandy said. "She knows better than to have the volume up that loud."

"What is it?" Plummy asked.

We all just stared at her. Even Romeo had been in the house long enough to feel itchy when he heard the music begin.

"It's *Willie Wonka and the Chocolate Factory,*" Little Tony said.

"Oh!" Plummy said. "The one with the blond guy? The one with the curls? I've always wanted to see that movie. Don't you want to watch it?"

"I've seen it," he said in perfect deadpan.

"Well, I'm going downstairs. I've been working all day, and I'm ready for a little mindless entertainment." Plummy kissed her father and left us there.

"My own sister," Big Tony said. "I feel I have a responsibility to keep her from getting sucked into the vortex."

Sandy shook her head. "She's already lost. There's no saving her now."

But the two Tonys went as well. Somehow the novelty of Plummy never having seen the movie made you want to go and watch her watch it. It was like bringing an Amish child into Times Square. She was so pure, so uncorrupted, that it was hard to resist being there to see it all fall apart.

"You should at least go downstairs and show Nora your arrangement."

"Nora has no interest in my arrangement." Sandy had studiously avoided her sister since she had taken up residence in the living room. She didn't do it in a way that anyone else would notice, but I saw it. She stayed at work longer. She made herself busier in the kitchen, she took it upon herself to fold all the laundry, she read the children an extra story at night. She was perfectly nice to Nora, and when it was incumbent upon her to fetch one thing or another she always did so with kindness and efficiency, but mostly Sandy was making herself scarce.

"Listen, anybody is going to go crazy over this arrangement, even your pregnant and slightly self-involved older sister."

"Not a chance."

"It's so different raising boys," Romeo said from the comfortable vantage point of the bed. "When they were growing up, one of my boys would get put out with one of his brothers and he'd just walk right up and punch him. Bang. No discussion. Then they'd roll around on the floor like a couple of rabid squirrels until someone got tired or hurt, and the whole thing would be over. Nobody could even remember what started it."

"So that's when they were kids. What about when they were adults?" Sandy was interested in conflict resolution.

Romeo said, "That's when they were adults, too."

"Well, you can't throw a punch at a pregnant woman who's lying in bed, even if she is your sister. It's simply not done."

"I respect that," Romeo said.

"But if you're curious, come downstairs and I'll show you what will happen." Sandy picked up her slender, splendid vase.

"I can't come downstairs," Romeo said. "Take your mother."

"I'm sorry," Sandy said. "I keep forgetting."

"I'm like the crazy wife Mr. Rochester kept in the attic. I live up here."

"What was a tough Italian boy doing reading *Jane Eyre?*" I asked.

"I was a tough Italian boy who worked in a flower shop. Now go on downstairs with Sandy."

I had never worried about Romeo being lonely before, and now I suddenly felt bad about leaving him. I must have had some sort of hangdog expression on my face because Romeo pointed firmly at the door, and said, "Go!"

No one gave a second thought to moving things around anymore. People pushed and dragged the furniture into new configurations depending on the size of the crowd. Tonight we had a full house, and everyone was just trying to find a comfortable place to sit.

Alex and Nora were in the hospital bed eating Chinese food out of paper cartons. It was not beneath my notice that Nora demanded only the purest, healthiest, and most expensive food from me, then would joyfully devour all the pizza and Thai food and cheeseburgers that Alex brought home for her at night. "It's a craving," she would explain. "I'm entitled."

Big Tony and Plummy and little Tony squeezed in together on the sofa while Sarah stretched out on the floor, watching the screen with all the intensity of a first timer. It was Plummy who saw us come in. After only a few minutes she had been able

to figure out how boring the movie was going to be, the genius girl.

"Nora, Alex, look. Look at Sandy's arrangement I was
telling you about."

"We're watching the movie," Nora said.

"Of course you are," Sandy said, and put the vase down on
the table.

Dear Alex, eternally oblivious to undercurrents, over cur-
rents, or repetition, lowered his chopsticks from his mouth.
The flowers caught him off guard. "Sandy, you *made* that?"

"I did," she said. Big Tony looked up and smiled at her.

"Nora, you've got to see this."

"I'm *watching* the *movie*. Be quiet." She kept her eyes on the
screen as if it were the final moments of a close presidential
election, and not a shot of poor Charlie Bucket being humili-
ated in his classroom for only being able to buy one Wonka bar.

In Nora's defense, she was not such a monster when Sandy
wasn't around, nor was Sandy as needy and pathetic when Nora
wasn't around. Quite often when the two of them came together they could be thoughtful and kind, or they could simply
resume a fight they were having in the backseat of the station
wagon thirty years ago: Her finger is on my side! She won't stop
looking at me! Mom, she's making faces at me! She took my

doll (book, coat, Oreo, whatever)! She's touching me! She said a bad word! Mom, MAKE HER STOP!

"Nora, for God's sake, you've seen the movie about a million times. Now turn your eyes to your sister's spectacular achievement." Alex's voice had an edge of incredulity. "I feel like I could dive into that thing and just swim in it."

No one was used to seeing Alex rock the boat. He was a tax attorney, after all, not a litigator. He was also the most devoted of husbands, but the flowers held him in their sway. The longer Nora went without looking, the more he insisted that she look, and the more he insisted, the more lockjawed she became.

At that point Nora was the only person in the room still watching the television set, and even she knew she was acting crazy, but she was in too deep to stop. Nora had no personal experience in backing down.

Still, if it were a boxing match, I'd have to say that Sandy won. She got her big compliment from Alex, while also proving her point that she was clairvoyant where her sister was concerned.

"I'm going home," Alex said, and swung his legs off the bed. "Nora, good night. Everyone, good night."

Then Nora's eyes finally did break free from the picture. "Why are you going home?"

"I'll call you later," he said, and got his suit jacket from where it was hanging off the back of the bed.

"Is this because I didn't look at Sandy's flowers? There, I'm looking. Gosh, they look nice. Now will you just sit back down?"

"Let's not wreck everybody's evening," Alex said.

"I didn't wreck the evening. I'm not the one who came in here when everybody was perfectly happy watching a movie and demand that they all stop what they were doing so they could praise me."

"What?" Sandy said.

"It's always about Sandy and her feelings. I'm the one who's pregnant!"

Sandy came around to the side of the bed. Big Tony took her hand, but she shook him off. "And when I was pregnant, I wasn't even allowed to talk about it in front of you. It was too boring. I was too conventional. But when *you're* pregnant, that's another story entirely, isn't it? When *you're* pregnant you build a shrine to yourself in the middle of the living room, where every single person who walks into the house has to come by and pay honor to your fertility."

"Okay, girls, that's enough." I said it in my mother's voice, the one I used when I looked back in the rearview mirror and threatened to pull the car over to the side of the road.

Nora was crying now. In some unimaginable world of hormonal high jinx, Nora had started crying before her sister.

"*I'm* the one who's sick," she said. "Everything was easy for you."

And just as Sandy opened her mouth for a hot retort, Sarah produced a sound so bloodcurdling, so beyond terrifying, that I thought there must be a stranger in the room with an axe and he'd chopped off Sarah's foot. She screamed and screamed and screamed.

Sandy leapt for her, and Nora sat up. We made a tight circle around the child, but she could not stop, no matter how many questions we asked.

"Where does it hurt?" "What did you see?" "Tell us, Sarah, tell us!"

She screamed and screamed again, and Sandy tried to hold her, but she could not be held. She flailed and fought and screamed. It couldn't have been more than thirty seconds, but it felt like days.

Then suddenly Romeo was in the room. He had run down the stairs without a thought when he heard such screaming. When his eyes searched the room, they landed on the television set. Willie Wonka was gone, and in his place there was Dawn Hayes with her perfect serene smile, an outline of the state of Massachusetts, and a row of numbers. It was Romeo who knew what had happened.

"Sarah, you won," he said.

With those words, he broke the spell. The screaming stopped, and she flew across the room to him, so grateful that finally someone had understood what she meant. In a single bound of joy, she leapt up into his arms.

And he caught her.

Chapter Twelve

EVERY LIFE IS A ROAD FULL OF FORKS: YOU CHOOSE and you choose and you choose and so your life is shaped. I married Mort Roth when I probably could have married someone else, someone I could have loved more and been happier with, but with that man I never would have had my daughters. Of course there could have been different daughters, but I have to say that whatever difficulties my girls have presented me, I have never been interested in trading them in. Since I cannot wish away Mort without wishing away Nora and Sandy, I will not wish away Mort.

Take Sandy. She could have married Tony in high school the first time they were in love, but instead Romeo and I broke them up and Sandy went on to marry the very dull Sandy Anderson and have Little Tony and Sarah, only to have a second chance to fork back to Big Tony in the end.

Nora waited until forty to get pregnant, but who knows how everything would have changed if she'd gotten pregnant twenty-three years ago (when I used to sit up nights worrying about exactly that)?

Leave the house at 9:00 in the morning and meet the love of your life at the T-stop. Leave the house at 9:05 and get run over by a car. There's simply no way to know in advance what the long-term outcome of a decision will be, no way of knowing how things might have turned out had you taken the other path. All the choices you make are knotted together, and you can't throw out the mistakes, and even if you could, you'd be unraveling the fabric of time. All the wonderful benefits that came as a direct result of an error would vanish as well. Live without regret, that's what my father taught me, and I believe him. You get one life, and every day you make a million choices, most of them too small to notice, but they shape you, all of them, and there's nothing you can do but go with it.

I wasn't supposed to buy another lottery ticket. I had made a solemn vow. But then Sarah felt so crummy and I felt so crummy for her that I turned the cart around. Was that fate? Only in retrospect.

Sarah had stopped screaming and Romeo had started. When she jumped onto his chest, propelled by the joy of the winning ticket, he went down like a house of cards.

Maybe the thing to do would have been to leave him there on the floor, at least until somebody called Dominic, or maybe we could have put him in the hospital bed next to Nora. Not a good solution long-term, but for that instant it would have been a reasonable choice. Nobody knew what the right thing was. We were all in the throes of our own separate, multilayered panics. So when Big Tony spoke clearly, we listened.

"We have to get him into bed," he said. "Alex, help me." And in two seconds they had lifted him, wracked and writhing in pain, and taken him right back up the stairs to deposit him in my bed. Poor Romeo had made his big escape only to end up exactly where he started.

When Tony ran in with the pain pills and a glass of water it was clear that swallowing was not an option. Before there was time to think of what to do next, Alex was on the phone calling Dominic for a shot. He was completely calm—unlike Big Tony, who was trembling as he stroked his father's head: unlike me, who was weeping as I held Romeo's hand: unlike the entire crowd who followed up the stairs and into the bedroom, leaving only Nora behind to float on her solitary raft in the living room.

"Daddy?" Plummy said, great tears balanced on the edges of her dark lashes.

In came Sandy, who had in less than a minute shifted gears

from thinking Sarah was dying to discovering Sarah won the Mass Millions (a fact that was completely lost in the shuffle, but I imagined would reemerge at a later time) to thinking Romeo was dying. She was wild-eyed, breathless.

"Romeo?" she said. She put her hand on one of his feet. There was so much tenderness in her voice it made me cry harder, remembering those far-off days in which she had hated him.

But Romeo wasn't answering anybody. He had retreated into his vertebrae, focusing so purely on his pain that I doubt he heard us at all. He was rigid again, gray again, once again his eyes rolled back.

Little Tony put his arms around his mother's waist and sobbed. Romeo had let him lie beside him in the bed every day, and together they'd read the sports page by holding it directly over their faces. They talked about baseball and planned a trip to go see a cave in New Hampshire once Romeo was up and around again. Tony cried like Romeo was dead.

"He's going to be fine," I said, trying to pull myself together. I wiped my eyes on the sleeve of my shirt and sat up straight. "This is just like the last time. He got better the last time, and he'll get better this time, too."

Sarah stayed a safe distance away from the bed, but her eyes were fixed on Romeo. "Did I kill him?" she finally asked her mother.

"You didn't kill him," Sandy said. "You just forgot not to jump up." The children, like puppies, had been drilled on the hazards of jumping up, and like puppies, they never remembered when they were excited.

Little Tony removed his face from his mother's shirt and turned to look at his sister. I thought he was going to say something awful, but after a minute all he did was look away from her, which seemed worse.

Plummy put her hands on Sarah's shoulders. "Come on, we should go downstairs. There are too many people in here, and we're sucking up all the air."

"I want to stay," Sarah said.

"Well, so do I, but that's not what's best for Daddy, so we're going to go. Anyway, we can't leave Nora down there all by herself." When Plummy and Sarah got to the door, they noticed that nobody was following them. "Come on," she said. "He's fine with Julie. We'll all go downstairs and wait for Dominic."

Despite her irrefutable logic, no one in the room was moving toward Plummy. Finally, there was a very small, very strained voice in the room, and Romeo said, "Go."

The oracle had spoken. The oracle, though damaged, was not dead. Alex and Sandy and Big Tony and Little Tony filed down the stairs behind Plummy and Sarah, and for a minute

Romeo and I were alone. I lay down very carefully in the bed beside him. I had become something of an expert at stretching out without causing the slightest bounce in the mattress. I put my hand very gently on his wrist.

"I have to tell you I'm feeling a little guilty about this," I said. "I felt guilty enough the last time, what with you carrying me up the stairs, but this time is almost as bad. I wanted you to stay with me. You kept getting better and better, and I was glad you were getting better, I was thrilled, but at the same time I didn't want you to go. I know if you were talking, you'd tell me that it wasn't my fault, but I don't know. I think I've been hanging out with Sarah too much. This whole business of wishing for things and wanting things is starting to catch up with me."

Romeo moved his fingers and I slipped my hand beneath his so he could press down on it. As bleak as things looked, I wasn't afraid this time. I'd seen him pull out of this before, and I had no doubt that he was able to do it again.

Then I remembered something crazy. Sarah had won the lottery. Or maybe she didn't win. No one had checked the numbers. It seemed completely possible that there had been a mistake.

I closed my eyes for a minute. There were just too many things to hold in my head, and all of a sudden I felt unbelievably tired. We stayed just like that on the bed, me and Romeo, our hands not exactly holding but certainly touching, until Dominic arrived.

"You two been at it again?" he said.

"It wasn't me." I opened my eyes and saw Dominic at the foot of the bed holding a syringe.

"They told me he made it downstairs. It must have been a big night."

"You could say that."

"I don't know whose bright idea it was to bring him back upstairs. If he was downstairs it would make some sense to take him into the hospital."

"There was a lot of confusion at the time. You should just move in. It would save you all the driving back and forth."

Dominic swabbed Romeo's hip and pushed the needle in. "If you asked on the right day, I'm sure my wife would be very pleased." He capped the needle and threw it back in the bag. "How's your head?"

"My head's fine, why?" I asked.

"Because you fell off a chair a couple of days ago. Do you remember that?"

"Oh Dominic, you know how it is—one crisis just obliterates the one that came before it. If it didn't happen today, I don't remember it."

"That's probably a very smart way to live," he said.

It looked as though no one had said anything to Dominic about the ticket, and when I walked him to the door the entire family was still sitting in the living room, looking like they had each swallowed his or her own individual mouse and were trying to keep their mouths closed for fear it would pop right back out again.

"How are you feeling, Nora?" The question seemed at once both neighborly and doctorly.

"Oh great," she said, giving him her best smile. "Super."

"Well, my hat's off to you. I'd have a hard time staying still."

"Romeo's my role model."

"He certainly should be. He's not going anywhere for awhile."

Big Tony stood up and came toward us. "Is he any worse?"

"Worse than where he started from? Probably not. It would be impossible to tell without an X-ray, but my best guess is that he reinjured the same spot. He's just going to have to wait for it to heal, and when it does heal he needs to stop picking people up."

Sarah dropped her head and looked very earnestly at her fingers.

He turned for the door, but no one said as much as goodbye. "You're an awfully quiet group tonight," Dominic said.

"We're just worried about Dad," Plummy said.

"Your father's going to be fine. I'll send Al over in the morning to check on him." He gave us all a wave and was gone.

"We have to send him some flowers," Plummy said.

"So who bought the ticket?" Sandy said. I had a feeling it wasn't the first time she'd asked the question. She was looking right at Nora.

"How could I have bought the ticket?" Nora said. "You know exactly where I've been all week."

Sarah just kept her eyes down. I didn't think she was capable of holding out against too much pressure for very long, but I found it admirable that she was trying.

"I bought the ticket." While I knew I wasn't supposed to, it seemed possible, just possible, that what I had done could be considered a good thing.

"I know it wasn't you," Sandy said dismissively.

"Why?"

"Because we talked about it. I asked you not to."

"But I did it anyway. I went behind your back. Why would I lie about it?"

"To protect Nora."

"That's great," Nora said, throwing up her hands. "I didn't do it, I have the perfect alibi, there's a credible confession, and still I'm getting blamed."

"It's a winning lottery ticket, not a parking ticket," Alex said. "I would think you'd be fighting each other to take the credit."

"I bought it," Little Tony said. "Sarah made me."

"Grandma bought it," Sarah said, then she ran over to me and held my arm. "I'm sorry."

I petted her hair. She would be the only eight-year-old in history punished for bringing millions into the house. "It's okay. Don't you remember? I made you promise not to tell, and you said you'd have to tell if you won. So you won. That was the deal."

"How could you have done that?" Sandy said.

"Really," Big Tony said in the alliance of son-in-laws, "I'm with Alex on this one. This is good news. I don't think we can even absorb the level on which this is good news."

Sandy had no intention of letting me go so easily. "But I specifically asked you not to. You knew it wasn't what was best for Sarah, you knew how I felt."

"Give it a rest," Nora said. "You bought her plenty of tickets yourself even after you knew you should stop. You were telling us not to buy her tickets, and you were still buying them. We all did it because it made her happy, which made us happy. Sarah, when Grandma bought you that ticket at the store last week, did it make you happy?"

Sarah was thoughtful, remembering that happiness and comparing it to what was happening now. She was extremely cautious. She was half-afraid her mother would take the ticket away from her or rip it up to prove a point. "It really did."

"And Mother, did it make you happy to buy Sarah the ticket?"

I nodded. "She had come home sick from school, and I just wanted to cheer her up. I loved buying her the ticket."

"There you have it: a child's happiness and a grandmother's happiness," Nora said, holding out her hand in Sarah's direction. "I rest my case."

Plummy sighed. "This is too much excitement for me. I'm going to go home to get some sleep. No matter what happens, I have a lot of flowers to get out in the morning."

"Don't you want to stay and see how the drama unfolds?" her brother asked.

"I'm sure I can find out tomorrow. Sarah?"

Sarah looked at Plummy and blinked.

"Do you mind if I borrow your movie? I want to watch the rest of it over at Dad's."

"Sure," Sarah said.

Plummy walked over to the VCR and punched the EJECT button as if this were the most natural thing in the world. "Thanks," she said. "I'll bring it back. Be sure to give Dad my love whenever he wakes up. Tell him I'll come by and see him tomorrow."

And with that, we witnessed the most remarkable event of the day: *Willie Wonka* left the building. Without Plummy, without the never-ending chorus of Oompah-Loompahs, the house seemed remarkably empty.

"Where's the ticket?" Sandy said.

"In my shoe."

"It's still in your shoe?" I asked. I couldn't believe that all this time had passed without anybody asking to see it, without anybody, including Sarah, checking to make sure she was right.

Sarah nodded. Sandy held out her hand, and Sarah dutifully unlaced her shoe and pulled out a flattened piece of aluminum foil—which couldn't help but call to mind if not a golden ticket, than at least a silver one. She gave it to her mother: then Sandy, without so much as opening the foil to see if there was a ticket inside, walked across the room and handed it to me.

"Why?" I said.

"You bought it. It's your ticket."

"It's Sarah's ticket. I bought it for her."

"Children can't play the lottery, and if they can't play, then they can't win, so you're just going to have to figure out what to do with it."

I tried to give it back to her. "You're Sarah's mother. If she can't have it, then it's your ticket."

Sandy held up her hands. I had a feeling she wasn't going to budge on this one.

"This is perfect," Nora said. "It's classic. We've raised good fortune to the level of Greek tragedy. Now, I want to go to bed. Go, all of you. I've had enough. Good night, family."

"Okay," Sandy said. "Tony, Sarah, go upstairs and brush your teeth. I'll be up in a little while to read to you."

"But this isn't a regular night," Sarah said.

I have to say I thought she had a point.

"The lottery won't protect you from cavities. Go."

So Tony and Sarah said good night, good night, good night. They kissed Alex and Nora and Big Tony. They came to kiss me. Sarah squeezed my neck for a minute and whispered in my ear. "Don't lose it."

"Promise," I said. They were slow to climb the stairs. They both kept looking back at us until finally Sandy pointed a finger, and they disappeared.

Alex came back in the room holding the newspaper. "Just in case anybody's interested, if that ticket is the winner and the only winner, it's worth seven and a half million dollars."

I had an overwhelming desire to get rid of the thing in my

hand. Seven and a half million should not be masquerading as an oversized stick of chewing gum. "Sandy, please."

I saw a little bit of sympathy cross the face of my youngest daughter. "I don't know what to do. It's scary. I feel like everything's going to change."

"It is," Nora said quietly. "For the better."

It was all Sandy needed, a little bit of compassion from her sister. I could almost see the tension dropping out of her shoulders. "Just keep it tonight," she told me. "We'll figure out what to do about it in the morning."

I walked upstairs holding on to the silver ticket, pinching it tightly by one corner. Romeo was out cold when I went into the bedroom. His face was relaxed, painless in its deep, chemical sleep, and I leaned over and kissed him gently on his sweet, slack lips. Nothing in him stirred.

I went around and sat down on the other side of the bed and very carefully peeled back the edges of the foil. There it was, the Massachusetts State Lottery, Mass Millions, and a row of numbers that either were or were not the ones that Sarah had seen on TV—although if I had to guess, I would say that this was a child who did not make mistakes where the lottery was concerned. Behind the ticket was a piece of cardboard cut out from the side of a box of Kix cereal. Wisely, she had thought that such a flimsy piece of paper would need a little bit of additional support. I thought of how this ticket had spent the week between her sock and the sole of her shoe, how it stayed with her through every step, down the hallways of school, out to the playground, walking home from the school bus and up the stairs to her room. It looked worn but not faded, and she was smart for wrapping it up.

Seven and a half million dollars.

Charlie Bucket had never dreamed of such a fortune.

Chapter Thirteen

I WAS DREAMING OF TICKETS, HUNDREDS OF THOUSANDS of tickets blowing around me in every direction. I was walking down the street in front of my house, and the tickets were coming straight toward me. They stuck between the branches of trees and clotted up underneath the shrubs. The wind pushed them into my clothes and tangled them in my hair, but they weren't frightening or overwhelming. They were like butterflies, harmless and light.

Then Sarah was there in her nightgown, following me out into the street. She was twirling around in the snowstorm of paper, and she said, "Grandma, Grandma, where's our ticket?" And at that moment I realized I was holding the winning ticket in my hand, and as soon as I saw it, I startled and let it go. The winning ticket spun away among all the thousands of identical losing tickets, and Sarah started running after it and I started running after Sarah, then Romeo came limping down the street, wanting me to wait for him. He kept calling me, "Julie! Julie!" and I didn't know what to do—run for the ticket or the child or the man with the bad back.

"Julie?"

"Hm?"

"You awake?"

"I am." I rubbed my eyes, and the tickets vanished. "Are you? Are you okay?" The room was dark, and I reached over and caught his hand. I slid my other hand into my pillowcase and patted around until I felt the sharp edge of tinfoil. Safe.

"My back is killing me."

"I bet it is. I'll get you a pill."

"What happened?"

"I was dreaming."

"No, what happened before that?"

"Last night?"

"All I remember," Romeo said, his words still fuzzy with Demerol, "is some terrible screaming. Horrible screaming. I thought that someone had broken in or the house was on fire. I ran downstairs and someone tackled me, then I woke up back here."

"That's it?"

"Pretty much."

I looked at the clock—4:00 A.M. "Sarah won the lottery."

"That's so weird. I had exactly the same dream."

"No, she really won. She was screaming and you ran downstairs and she jumped on you."

Romeo was quiet for a minute, trying to put it all together. "Right," he said finally.

"Let me get you a pill before things get worse."

With all the progress Romeo had made in his recovery, we had outgrown the bendy-necked straws. They had made their way back to the kitchen, so I put on my bathrobe and went to find them. It felt like old times. I went down the stairs in complete silence. It was an old house, but it was my old house, and I knew where every creak and groan was waiting. I stepped from right to left, left to right, and passed over the fifth step altogether.

When I passed the living room, there was enough light coming in from the streetlight that I could see Nora and Alex asleep in the hospital bed, his arms around her shoulders, her head on his chest, any trace of an argument long forgotten. They made a very sweet picture. I crept off and found the straws and made it upstairs undetected. I felt like an especially nimble domestic superhero.

"How much?" Romeo asked, when I came back into the room.

"Seven and a half million if there are no other claims on the ticket."

He tried to whistle, but he lacked the fine motor skills. "That's the mother lode of Barbies, all right."

I laughed at this, trying to picture what seven and a half million dollars of Barbie flesh would look like. One thing's for certain, they'd all be wearing fur coats. "I don't think we'll just turn all the money over to her right away."

"How will Sandy do it?"

"I have no idea. We didn't talk about it. First, we had to make sure that you weren't dead, and Dominic came over and gave you a shot, then Sandy got mad at me for buying the ticket."

"You bought the ticket?"

"I was on strict orders not to, but then, I don't know, I just caved."

"I hardly think it's something to feel bad about. I've bought her lots of tickets. I'd be pretty pleased with myself if one of them had won."

"Yes, but you didn't buy them after the No Ticket Edict had been issued."

"Sandy will get over it."

"I'm sure you're right. And after that, we'll figure out what we're going to do with the money."

Romeo opened his mouth like a dear little bird, and I dropped the pill down his gullet and gave him a sip of water. "It's very good," he said.

"Try to get some sleep."

"I guess I'm not going anywhere for awhile."

"That's the good news."

"Really?" He was turning his head in quarter-inch increments, trying to see me, so I leaned forward until my nose was directly over his nose.

"Really." I kissed him good night. Again.

❧

Romeo was right. In the morning, I met Sandy in the kitchen, and she came and put her arms around me first thing. "We didn't get a lot of sleep last night."

"No," I said. "Neither did we."

"Tony and I talked all night. He thought I behaved badly to you, and he's right. I wasn't looking at the bigger picture. You broke the rule, but certainly something very good came out of that. I wasn't thinking clearly."

"It was a lot to take in. And I should have listened to you."

"I actually don't think this is going to turn Sarah into a gambling addict."

"Well, if we're operating on the Wonka principle, Charlie Bucket didn't come home asking for a second golden ticket."

"And seeing as how our entire life operates on the Wonka principle, I guess we pretty much know what to expect."

Sarah and Little Tony came into the kitchen quietly. Everyone was quiet in the morning now, and everyone shut the doors behind them. We all knew that Nora asleep was easier to manage than Nora awake, so we wanted her to sleep for as long as possible.

"Good morning," Little Tony said.

"I'm rich," Sarah said. The smile on her face was enormous. Clearly she had had some time to think about it, too.

"Is this the way it's going to be from now on?" Tony said resentfully. "I'm rich, I'm rich, I'm rich?"

"Yes," Sarah said.

"No," Sandy said. "Listen to me, both of you. You are to tell absolutely *no one* at school about this. Do you understand me? No one. We don't know what we're going to do with the ticket yet. We don't need every news channel in the state camped out on our front steps."

"You think I'll be on television?" Sarah gave a frightfully coy smile.

"Here it comes," Tony said.

"No," Sandy said, trying her best to sound stern, but I could tell she also wanted to laugh over the whole thing. "You will not be on television. We're going to handle this with as much dignity and privacy as is humanly possible."

"Where's my ticket?"

"I have it," I told her.

"But where is it? It's mine. I want to see it."

"Sarah, you're on thin ice here. Don't talk that way to your grandmother. As far as I'm concerned and as far as *the law* is concerned"—she tried to make the idea of law sound as threatening as possible—"that ticket belongs to her, so be respectful."

"I'm sorry," she said. "May I see it, please?"

Actually, the ticket was conveniently located in the pocket of my bathrobe. I hadn't thought of the absolutely best place for it yet, and until I did, I planned to keep it on my person. That dream had shaken me up. I handed it to Sarah, tinfoil and all.

She took it carefully between two fingers, as if it might be hot, or as if I might try and snatch it back from her. "I just want to show you in the paper."

Alex had left the paper folded on the table to the page that ran the lottery numbers. Sarah carefully unwrapped the foil and removed her ticket. She placed it on top of the paper and read the numbers aloud. "They're 1-17-33-39-44-46, Bonus number: 7." And then she screamed again.

I leapt on her in a split second and clamped my hand over

her mouth. "Don't scream! You're going to have Romeo running down the stairs again, and this time it might really be trouble."

Sandy slumped down in a chair and then dropped her head onto the table. Every number matched. The bonus number matched.

"Do I have to go to school today?" Sarah asked.

"Yes," Sandy said.

Tony leaned over to look at the paper, and Sarah grabbed up her ticket like he might try and touch it. "Wait a minute," Tony said. "That's a Mass Millions ticket. You never play Mass Millions. You only play Mega Millions."

"I know. Grandma bought it."

"And those aren't your numbers. Not one single one of them. You've never played those numbers before in your life."

"Grandma got a quick pick." She didn't see where this was going.

"So you *aren't* lucky! It isn't your game, and they aren't your numbers! If you'd had your way, you would have kept losing forever. It *is* Grandma's ticket, and she doesn't owe you a dime of the money."

"It's mine because she bought it for me. It's totally mine."

Sandy plucked up the ticket and handed it back to me. Sarah looked poised to wail, but her mother cut her off. "Both of you, voices down, now. We've got a houseful of sick, sleeping people, and what they're going through is a lot more important than any scrap of paper. My peace of mind isn't worth seven and a half million dollars, so don't push me. You will eat your breakfasts quietly, you will take your lunch sacks to school, and you will keep your mouths shut all day. Do I make myself clear?"

"Yes," Tony said quietly.

Sarah waited a beat. There was a glimmer of real defiance in her eyes, the kind I used to see in Nora when she was little. Sandy just stared her down. "Yes," Sarah said finally.

"I'm glad we understand each other."

It was snowing outside, not a hard snow but a pretty, dusting snow that caught the light and shone. I made the oatmeal, and Sandy made turkey sandwiches.

"Remember, no mustard," Sarah said.

Sandy turned around holding a slice of bread in her hand. "You've never eaten mustard. In all the years I've known you, you've never even tried mustard. I'm your mother. Do you think I would have forgotten that fact?"

"I was just reminding you," Sarah said sullenly.

Little Tony picked up the paper and folded it to the comics page. "I want that lottery page," Sarah said, grabbing. And Tony, who was satisfied to see his sister so thoroughly chastised, tore it off and gave it to her with no fuss at all.

"What are you going to do with that?" Sandy asked.

"I want to save it," she said. "If I can't have the ticket, then at least I can have this."

Sandy thought about it for awhile and agreed. "Okay, but it's just for you. Don't go showing it to the kids at school."

I bundled everyone up in mittens and hats, distributed lunch sacks and kisses, and sent them on their way.

"You'll take good care of it?" Sarah asked, like she was leaving her first hamster in my custody.

I nodded and kissed them all good-bye. When they were gone, I took the ticket out of my pocket and carefully wrapped it back in its foil envelope. It felt absolutely essential, like the numbers might change if I didn't put it back exactly as I had found it. It occurred to me that Sarah probably did have a real streak of obsessive-compulsive disorder and that that disorder might be contagious.

Nora called out from the living room, "Mother!"

I poured her a glass of Evian, cold, no ice, and took it in to her.

Nora pulled herself up in the bed. She was like one of those amazing time-lapse films that the Nature Channel shows, with the little seed pushing up from the ground and shooting off a stem and green leaves, then a bud and a flower and a full bloom, all in a matter of a minute. Every morning, I thought she had doubled in size from the night before.

"Can I even tell you how much I miss coffee?" she said.

"I can't even imagine it. Back when I was pregnant we didn't have to give anything up, we just had to cut back a little: two glasses of wine, ten cigarettes a day. Coffee was essentially considered to be dark tap water."

"A little knowledge is a dangerous thing." She drank her water down in one long gulp and handed me back the glass. "Thank you."

"I'll get your breakfast."

"Wait, tell me how Romeo is. Should I call him?"

"I'd wait until tomorrow. I don't think he's going to be answering the phone today. He's pretty bad off."

"And the littlest Rockefeller?"

"Already gone to school."

"I can see it now: Sarah gets elected homecoming queen and captain of the basketball team and the cheerleading team and student body president, while all of her new little friends line up at the door to see if we give cash advances against allowances."

"Except that Sandy told both of the kids not to tell anyone about it."

"Sarah told every kid in school she was going to win the lottery. Do you really think she's not going to tell them, now that she actually has?"

"I'm just hoping that Sandy was sufficiently threatening to at least hold her off for a couple of days. I don't have any idea how Sandy's going to handle this, and Sandy seems to think it should be my decision since I'm the one who bought the ticket."

"What's there to handle?" Nora asked.

I sat down on the edge of the hospital bed. "Where to begin? Do we just put it all in a trust and give it to her when she's eighteen? Do we give it to her when she's thirty? Do we give her a little bit now? I have no idea. This wasn't a problem I had when you and your sister were growing up."

"You're really thinking we should just turn all the money over to Sarah?"

It was clearly a trick question, but I still wasn't getting it. "It's her money."

"So Sarah gets to go to Princeton and have a dorm named after her, and Little Tony goes to community college, works at Dunkin' Donuts, and lives at home?"

"I'm sure Sarah would help . . ." I said, but the words were not completely convincing even as they were coming out of my own mouth.

Nora lowered her eyebrows at me. "I know this is politically incorrect of me to point out, but Sandy and Big Tony are in fact poor people. They are smart people and kind people, but they have the financial planning abilities of goldfish. Big Tony's in school and wants to stay in for more school. I doubt that after his years in the Peace Corps and the World Health Organization he's earned more than sixty thousand dollars sum total over the course of his life. Sandy is still paying off the credit card bills she racked up in her first marriage. The only thing that keeps them from living in a one-bedroom apartment in Roxbury is you, and you're not exactly loaded yourself."

Nora was never one to beat around the bush.

"Little Tony, being a poor kid, is basically fine in this family dynamic, but now Sarah is a rich kid, and that changes everything. A rich kid cannot be raised by poor parents."

"You make it sound like she's going to be slicing truffles on her Cheerios in the morning while the rest of the family sits there sharing a piece of toast."

"It's not an entirely unlikely scenario. If she has all the money, she also winds up with all the power, and too much power never brought out the best in anybody, especially a strong-willed child. Why is she going to let Sandy tell her what to do if Sandy is poor?"

"Because she's her mother."

"In case you haven't noticed, that in and of itself is not enough to make a child listen."

"So how do you suggest we solve this problem?"

"It's perfectly clear: You give the money to all of them."

"But it's Sarah's ticket. How can we just decide arbitrarily to take it away from her?"

Nora shook her head. She was trying to exercise patience with me, but it was early, and she hadn't had any coffee. "There's nothing arbitrary about it. You, as the adult, are making the decision that will best protect the child—and this child will be best protected by not having things get completely out of whack in her family. They should buy a house, Tony should go to medical school, Sandy should buy a real car, both of the kids should have cello lessons and tennis lessons, and if they want to go to private schools, well, that's what money is for."

"You're making something that's very complicated sound very easy." I straightened up the covers and reached over and pushed the hair out of her eyes. "I appreciate that."

Nora smiled at me. "You're a really decent person, Mother. You have a big heart, and you always want to be fair. But families aren't democracies. You don't make your children feel good by giving them a fair say. You make your children feel good by protecting their better interests, regardless of what they want. What if Sarah wanted to spend seven and a half million on Pez?"

"Romeo said Barbies."

"You'd stop her. Tell me you'd stop her."

Maybe certain things skipped generations. Maybe Nora would turn out like my mother. She would never pick up a hula hoop; she would stand back and be distant and wise while her children came to my house to roll around on the floor with me like a pack of puppies.

"Help me up," Nora said. "I have to go to the bathroom."

Nora went to the bathroom a lot. She was allowed only the briefest trips out of bed, and every time her feet touched the floor, she teetered like a sailor who was standing on dry land for the first time in years. She could make it by herself, but she liked it when I held her hand and walked her all the way to the door.

I wondered about my mother. I know she would have done this for me, I know she would have taken care of me had I shown up at forty with an incompetent cervix that was trying to hold back triplets, but I don't know that I would have been able to ask her to hold my hand on the way to the bathroom, not when both of us knew I could have made it on my own. So maybe there wasn't one right way to be a mother. Maybe something about my sloppy, indulgent love had done some good.

I waited outside the door for Nora and walked her back to bed, then helped her get comfortable. "I'll wash your hair this morning," I said. "We'll get you a little bath while everybody's gone, then you'll be all straightened up again."

But Nora wasn't listening to me. When I looked at her, she had tears in her eyes. "What's wrong?" I said. "Does something hurt?"

She shook her head and put her hands on her belly. "I just hate getting up, is all. Every time I get up, I'm so afraid I'm going to lose them."

Chapter Fourteen

WITHIN A WEEK OF WINNING, SARAH HAD DISCOV-
ered the Post-it note. She now made notes to herself about
everything. After school, she immediately sat down with the
massive stacks of catalogs that found their way into our house
every day and marked all the items she was interested in. *I
WANT THIS* she would write, then stick the note on the page.
She preferred to write in red crayon or fat blue Magic Marker,
and what with all the capital letters and various-sized exclama-
tion points, she got her message across. Sometimes she managed to put a yellow sticky on every page so that the catalogs
were thick and wouldn't stack properly.

"You want sterling silver napkin rings?" I asked.

"My dolls can wear them as bracelets," she said. "You can
get them monogrammed, too, but I'm going to put my initials

on them, not the dolls, so I can use them for napkins when I grow up."

"Very canny." I kept flipping through. She wanted a chrome blender and heart-shaped cake pans and a Tiffany watch and patio furniture, despite the fact we had no patio.

"We will," she said cryptically.

"Men's shoes?"

"Those are for Romeo."

"That's thoughtful." I didn't tell her that Romeo wasn't a tassel sort of guy; what counted was the thought.

Catalogs, of course, can only offer a limited amount of what a girl wants. So Sarah took notes while she watched television, too. She wrote down all the things she was interested in having on the commercials—the Easy-Bake Oven, a Mac computer in orange—but she also jotted down the random things she saw on shows that caught her fancy: a red couch, a blue car. One note said simply: high-heeled shoes. These notes she would leave on the refrigerator next to the grocery list. Soon they were layered like shingles. She put them on every door in the house as gentle reminders of her every desire. What impressed me the most was what a good speller she was.

"This is full-on insanity," Sandy said, when Sarah presented her with a stack of catalogs the minute she walked in the door from work. "Do you think I'm going to sit down and order all of this for you just because you want it? You don't even have the money yet."

"Keep a list," Sarah said. "I'll pay you back."

"You won't pay me back because you can't have it. Even if you could afford it, I'm not going to just let you have every-thing you want." She slapped her hand down on the stack of catalogs, and they slid awkwardly to one side. "I did not raise you to be spoiled."

"There's plenty of stuff in there I'm going to buy for you," Sarah said, but I felt like the word *maybe* was lingering in the air, as in, *Maybe if you're good.*

"Go play with Aunt Nora," Sandy said darkly.

Sarah sighed the way rich people sigh when they talk about how hard it is to find good help these days.

"And you need to feed Oompah-Loompah and clean out her box. You haven't been taking care of her at all."

"Tony can feed her."

"She's your cat. You promised me that if I let you have a cat, you'd take care of her."

"When the money comes in, I'll hire someone for Oompah," she said. Then she fixed Nora a Pellegrino, twisted a piece of lime into the glass, and pushed out through the kitchen door.

"A cat nanny," I said.

"This could be an incredible gift," Sandy said, flipping

randomly through the marked items. "God is giving us a glimpse of the future. There's still time to throw the ticket away." She pointed to a glossy catalog page. "Look, she wants a mink bedspread."

"I don't think getting rid of the ticket is the answer."

"She wants luggage. She's even marked the color. She's eight, where's she going to go?"

"This is just some bizarre aberration. It's like letting a child into a chocolate factory."

Then Sandy and I looked at each other, and we broke up laughing.

For three days we held the line. It was a raging battle in which we neither progressed forward nor did we fall back. Sarah continued to submit her list of demands, and we continued to explain to her with varying degrees of patience why it just wasn't going to happen. Nora talked to Alex about the tax consequences, Sandy talked to Tony about the emotional consequences, I talked to Romeo about the possibility that someday there might be fewer people living in the house.

"I can see Sarah buying one of those big old four-stories in Cambridge, but I doubt she'd take her family with her," Romeo said. "So it might not thin out the traffic around here as much as you'd think."

No one knew what we were supposed to do. The only thing

we could all agree on was the fact that until we could agree on something, we shouldn't tell anyone about what had happened. I had always hated that scene in *Wonka* when Charlie first discovers he's found the last golden ticket. He gets mobbed on the street, people are all over the kid, and he's trying to protect his find by holding it up over his head, which is kind of silly, considering that he's a child surrounded by tall adults. It's amazing that someone didn't just rip it out of his hands and make a run for it.

As for me, I held on to the ticket until one day I spent an hour going through my pockets looking for it. I had a load of laundry in the washer, and I imagined Mass Millions going around and around in the hot, soapy water until every number had loosened its hold on the paper. I thought I would have to go to the emergency room with heart palpitations, when I finally found it in an old cardigan I had taken off and put back in the closet. That's when I called Gloria to come over and get me. My hands were shaking too much to drive.

"You're calling me for a ride to the bank?" she said.

"I need to visit the safety-deposit box. I'll tell you all about it when you get here."

Half an hour later I found Gloria sitting up on Nora's hospital bed, discussing the logistics of breast-feeding triplets.

"Give up now," Gloria said. "Before you start it. Give it up before you even really think about it too much."

"Other people have done it," Nora said. "I didn't invent the idea."

"No, but you can put a stop to it." She shuddered. "Do you want us to bring you anything weird, peanut butter ice cream maybe?"

Nora suddenly lit up like the North Star. "That sounds fantastic, actually." The farther along she got, the more she seemed to lose her way as far as her aggressively healthy impulses were concerned.

Gloria leaned over and kissed her. "I have to kiss you. You look so pretty!"

"I look like a house," Nora said.

"Darling, you *are* a house. Think of all the people you're sheltering. You're a very pretty house."

When our kids were growing up, I often considered sending Nora out to live with Gloria. They always knew how to talk to each other.

It was a lovely day, freezing cold and cloudy. Maybe it was just a lovely day because I was out of the house for a few minutes. I was like a little white terrier we had when I was a child, who lived for nothing but the privilege of riding in the car. Like Suzy, I wanted to roll the windows down and stick my nose into the wind.

"How's it going with Nora?" Gloria asked.

"It's okay. She's a handful, but that's no surprise."

"And Romeo?"

"He hurt his back again. I think he'll be in bed for a few more weeks now."

"Oh, Julie," she said, her voice brimming with sympathy. "I don't know how you manage."

I had been looking for the right moment, the proper way to break the news. Even though we were a family sworn to secrecy, I felt sure that everyone would agree that Gloria was a member of the family. "Actually, there's something else."

When I told Gloria the news about Sarah, she had to pull her car over to the side of the road to catch her breath. "This isn't something you want to tell a person when she's operating heavy machinery." She kept her hands gripped to the steering wheel.

"I made a point not to tell you over the phone. I wanted to be there in case you passed out."

"So you could install me in the Roseman Hospital?" Gloria took a deep breath, and after she had waited a reasonable amount of time, she flicked on her turn indicator and pulled back into traffic. "I wonder if I could adopt Sarah, become her legal guardian?"

"Gloria! What a thing to say."

"Well, she's going to torture you and Sandy from here on out. Maybe I'd have better luck, not being a blood relative."

"At this point we haven't decided to give her up, but I'll let you know."

We went into the little Somerville bank branch where I've been doing business forever. The bank has been bought and sold and merged half a dozen times since my parents first started taking me there, but it's always been the same building and many of the same people stay for years and years at a time. Not everybody knows the people in their bank, but if you own a small business, have gotten a divorce, and have gone through a couple of second mortgages, refinancing, and a few embarrassing bounced checks, you will.

"Hi, Julie!" one teller said.

"Hi, Jody," I called back to her.

"So you have *it* with you now?" Gloria whispered.

"Discussion *verboten*," I said in a low voice. "Sally, I'm going to need to get into my lockbox." I held up my key as if to show proof of my intentions.

"Sure, Julie, not a problem."

She opened the cage door, which I have always thought of as very stylish prison bars, and led us into the little room full of boxes. I don't know why going into my safety-deposit box always strikes me as a little bit melodramatic. I feel like I should be taking out a very large diamond or putting in a very small gun. She turned the keys, pulled out the long, thin box, and set it on the table.

"Are you going to be awhile?" Sally asked.

"Not at all." I reached into my pocket and slipped the tin-foil wrapper in the box, then I pushed the lid closed. "There, see? All done."

"That was nothing," Sally said, picking the box back up and sliding it in.

"A little more than nothing," Gloria said.

I was cutting Gloria a dirty look when Sally turned back around. "Julie, I have to tell you the funniest story. Maybe I shouldn't say anything, but it was so cute. I don't think we have confidentiality laws where kids are concerned."

"Kids?"

"Sarah, your granddaughter, she called here yesterday."

"She called you?"

"Actually no, I answered the phone, and she said she had to talk to the president. I gave her to Tommy." She told Gloria, "He's our branch manager."

"Sure," Gloria said, nodding.

"She said she wanted to know how much money you could put in a bank. Isn't that cute?"

"Darling," I said flatly.

"Tommy didn't understand what she was talking about. He kept telling her she could put in as much money as she wanted, and then she said, 'But what if I have more money than anybody else?' And Tommy tells her that would be fine, that we would take care of it for her. And she just keeps saying, 'You don't understand. What if it's a lot more money than you think?' She asks him how much money the richest person at this bank has and he tells her, 'I'm sorry, Sarah, we can't disclose that information.' So then she thanks him and hangs up."

Sally was really cracking herself up telling this one. Gloria and I tried to chuckle along here and there just to keep pace.

"I hope she wasn't too much of a bother," Gloria said. "It was for a school project she was working on. They're trying to help the children understand what it means to save, you know, as a concept larger than piggy banks."

"Sure," Sally said, and wiped a tear from the corner of one eye with her finger. "We thought it was something like that."

After our polite good-byes, Gloria and I ran back and got in the car. For some reason we locked the doors as if we were participating in some particularly nefarious activity. "How do you lie like that?" I asked her. "I could do it if I had some time, but you don't even blink. I'm so impressed."

"Years of practice," she said.

"If she's already called the bank, you have to wonder who else she's told."

As it happened, we did not have to wonder for long.

There was a car I didn't recognize parked in my driveway when I got home. When Gloria and I opened the door, Nora called out in a strange, small voice, "Mom?"

"Yes, it's Mom," I said, and then I walked into the room to find my ex-husband, his second wife, and a blond-headed two-year-old in my living room.

"Jules!" Mort said, standing up from the sofa to give me an awkward little half hug. "And Gloria, too. I should have known the old partners in crime would be out together."

"Hi, Mort," Gloria said, and gave him a brief peck on the cheek.

"Julie," Lila said tightly, and gave me a little nod. "Gloria."

"Lila," we said together. The last time Lila and I had occasion to be in the same room was not too long after Romeo and I started seeing each other. Mort and Romeo got into a fistfight that landed them both in the hospital awhile.

"This is Nicolette," Nora said, pointing to the little girl who was removing every file from the file boxes one at a time and putting them each in a different corner of the room. "Dad, she might not want to be doing that."

It was not a particularly Nora-like way of addressing a

problem, but we were all aware that this tiny person undoing all of her secretary's work was, in fact, her sister who she had never met before.

"Oh, she'll put 'em back." Mort called out to the child, "Honey, start putting those back now." Nicolette then started scooping the files up together pell-mell and cramming them upside down into a wastebasket. "See, she's close."

I looked at my watch. It was three o'clock; we still had a little time before Sandy picked the kids up from school. "I don't mean to be rude, but might I ask why you're visiting?" It was rude. There was no way around it. Maybe I even meant it as such.

Mort held out his open palm to Nora. "Do I need more of a reason than this? My firstborn baby girl is about to have triplets. I think that calls for a plane trip out from Seattle."

Suddenly Nicolette dropped all the files on the floor as if she had just been run through with a jolt of electricity. "SIPPY CUP!" she screamed. I almost jumped out of my shoes.

"Inside voice," Lila said lightly, while she rummaged through the toddler bag for a beverage. She came up with the cup but it was empty.

"SIPPY CUP SIPPY CUP SIPPY CUP!" Nicolette wailed. Lila cleared her throat. "Julie, do you have any apple juice?"

"Yes, I do." I started to stand up.

Lila looked at me with some hesitation. "I'm sorry, but is it organic, pesticide-free apple juice? You wouldn't believe what's in commercial apple juice these days."

Nora's head slipped limply to the side.

"Yes," I said politely. "I do. Gloria, would you show Lila the kitchen, please?"

"I'd really like that," Gloria said, then she looked down at the sack in her hands. "Oh, Nora, look, we remembered your ice cream. You don't want ice cream now, do you?"

"No," Nora said.

"I didn't think so. Come on, Lila, I'll show you the kitchen." The two of them left, with Nicolette close at their heels. "So how old were you when you had this baby?" I heard Gloria say just before the door shut.

Mort watched them disappear. "She's a great kid, really. But it's a hell of a flight. We took the red eye. Got on the plane just as soon as we heard the news."

"Nora only told you she was pregnant yesterday?"

Nora twisted in her hospital bed. "Mom, please, this is torture, and I'm not supposed to be tortured, okay? Sarah called Dad and told him about the ticket. They're here for the money."

"Oh, Nora," Mort said sadly. "That's not really what you think?"

"No bullshit, Dad—really, my nerves can't take it."

Mort chuckled to me. "Now she swears at her father. Kids."

There was a great toddler scream coming from the kitchen, then complete silence. Nora and I both flinched like a gun had gone off.

"You get used to it," Mort said. "Even at my age."

"I'm going to go upstairs and check on Romeo." I stood up and nodded. "Mort, always nice to run into you in my own living room."

"Cacciamani is living here? You married the bum, and no one told me?"

"I didn't marry him, he's not a bum, and no one would have told you because it wouldn't have been any of your business."

"But you've got him stashed away up in our bedroom? With kids around? I'm sorry Julie, that's not okay."

Lila and Gloria reemerged from the kitchen with Nicolette sucking her cup. She had that glassy-eyed stoned look kids get when they finally get the apple juice they've been wanting so badly.

"Nora, sketch things out briefly for your father while I go upstairs."

"Is everything okay?" Gloria said.

"I need to lie down before I have a heart attack," I said.

"If that's the case, then I'm going to leave, too. Nora, will you be okay?"

"Eventually," she said. "Probably."

I kissed Gloria good-bye. Lila stood there glowering at me in my own living room, and I turned away.

Mort had started to steam, something he did even when we were first married. He would get sweaty and red, then his eyebrows would start to twitch. "Don't walk away from me, Julie, I'm serious. There are little children living in this house, and I won't have you just bringing men in."

"Dad," Nora said. "Remember what I told you?"

"I respect your nerves, Nora, but this is very important," Mort said. "Listen, I'll pack Sandy and those two little children up and take them all out to Seattle with us, where at least they can live in a wholesome environment."

"Sandy's married now, Mort. Remember that? You missed the wedding. She's married to Tony Cacciamani, so be sure to take him with you, too."

Mort starting answering me, and Lila was still silent, but I went upstairs anyway. I actually felt bad for Nora. If I'd had the strength, I would have picked her up and carried her with me. But I didn't have the strength, not even a fraction of it.

I went into my bedroom and closed the door, then I just stood there. I felt completely unable to move.

"So here's what I've been able to deduce," Romeo said. "We have a lot of company, and they're not here to see me."

"Correct."

"There's a child with them, a girl, and she's a screamer. You'll notice I didn't run down the stairs this time."

"Excellent judgment."

"And it's someone you really don't like."

"Could you hear all of that?"

"I couldn't make out the words, but I could definitely pick up on your tone. Very clipped. I wouldn't want to be on the receiving end of that tone."

"As usual, you're right on all counts."

"Lying up here trapped in bed has made me something of a master sleuth. So who was it?"

I thought about making him guess, but I didn't think his recovery time was going to be that long. "Mort, Lila, and their new daughter, Nicolette."

"Mort Roth is downstairs?" I saw Romeo's arms jump up, and his head left the pillow for a split second before the pain caught up with him and dropped him back.

His face was flushed, and it reminded me unfortunately of Mort. Our families had pretty much managed to let go of the generations' worth of anger that had thrived between us, but chances were slim that Romeo and Mort were ever going to be pals. That was fine with me.

"So he just showed up in the living room with no warning?"

"He said they'd come to see Nora. They wanted to congratulate her on her exciting pregnancy."

Then his eyes grew round with disbelief. "He's come for the money!"

I picked up his hand and kissed it. "For someone who's doped up on pain pills, you still have an incredibly sharp mind. He thinks I'm an unfit grandparent. I have a man in my bedroom. He thinks that Sandy and Little Tony and, oh yes, Sarah, should come and live with them in Seattle. I have a hunch they're less than interested in taking along your son."

"And why can't I kill him?"

"Because you can't sit up by yourself."

Then Romeo started swearing, a long and creative string of expletives that had an unexpectedly soothing affect on me. I lay down in the bed next to him and closed my eyes while he put words together in a way I hadn't heard since high school. If he couldn't fight for my honor, he would certainly swear in my defense. It was sweet.

Chapter Fifteen

JUST BEFORE HE SLIPPED OFF TO SLEEP, I GAVE
Romeo a pain pill. Afterward I looked at the bottle long and
hard and wondered how it would be such a crime if I took one
or maybe just half of one, but I didn't do it. I had a cold suspicion that one pill this afternoon would mean I'd be selling the
television sets by noon tomorrow trying to support my habit.
It probably wasn't the time for self-medication.

I lay down beside Romeo and closed my eyes without feeling particularly restful. My mind was showing the greatest hits
of Nora and Sandy, whether I felt like watching them or not:
Nora and Sandy as babies, as sweet little girls, and as fearsome
teens. Nora and Sandy at various graduations, in bridal gowns,
in my kitchen at Thanksgiving, laughing. I would always take
in my daughters and their families. I would provide for them.

I would feed them and nurse them and love them, but I felt absolutely incapable of protecting them from their father.

Where Mort was concerned, they were on their own. After all, they loved him. They should love him. Whatever difficulties they had in their relationship were not for me to navigate. Wasn't it Nora, after all, who had called Mort when I was first dating Romeo, so that he could fly out here to break us up?

Now I was lying in my bed worrying about her having to deal with him alone. I was worried about Sandy, who would soon walk in the house and be ambushed by reports of my bad behavior. And not two minutes later, I heard the voices of the children downstairs. I could hear the stronger voices of adults. Like Romeo, I wasn't able to make out exactly who was saying what, but I could understand it wasn't good.

Then there was a knock on my door. The knock no longer asked a question, "Are you in there? May I come in?" The knock simply made a pronouncement, "Cover yourself! I'm coming in." Then Mort was standing in my bedroom.

Romeo didn't wake up, and maybe if I had taken the pill, I would be asleep myself. It wasn't a comforting thought to imagine Mort in my room while I was sleeping, but it was easier to manage than the thought of his being in there while I was awake.

"Out," I said. My mind could not extend to any thought more complicated than that.

Mort took it all in, the draperies and the table lamps and the chair in the corner with the needlepoint cushion. Everything was exactly as he had left it except that now Romeo was in the bed, asleep on what had once been Mort's side. "Oh Christ, I do hate the sight of this." He shook his head.

Romeo was under the covers in fully buttoned pajamas (though sadly, they were my pajamas, the flannel ones with the roses which he liked because they were softer than his) and I was completely dressed and on top of the covers with an afghan over my feet.

"Out, *out*," I said.

"In our own room. Our own bed! Julie, my mother made that afghan."

I kicked it off onto the floor. "Take it."

Sandy came in behind him, looking wild-eyed. "Mom, I tried to stop him."

"He can't be stopped." I closed my eyes and willed them all to go. When I opened my eyes again they had only doubled, then tripled. There was Lila with the bouncing Nicolette, there was Little Tony, and then, finally, here came Sarah. I tried again. "Oh come on people, really—out!"

Mort cleared his throat and pinned on his best smile. "Sarah said she didn't want us to be mad at each other anymore."

"Super," I said. "We won't be. Go."

"I want all my grandparents together," Sarah said.

"And so we are," Mort said. "Which is just great. Everybody is getting along."

Sarah started hopping up and down, up and down, clapping her hands together.

"Hey, settle down. Romeo is sleeping. You know he needs to get his rest."

"It's just like the movie," Sarah said excitedly. "It's just like Charlie's house."

It was nothing like the Bucket house. Poor Charlie Bucket lived in a shack, and his downtrodden mother, the washerwoman, took care of her parents and her husband's parents, the four of whom shared a big bed together in the middle of the living room. The two impossibly ancient couples faced each other, one at each post of the four-post bed, their feet poking up beneath the single cover. There was not the slightest whiff of any funny business going on. The sight of them all piled up together like that was any caretaker's worst nightmare.

"I want you like the movie," Sarah said.

"Like *Willie Wonka and the Chocolate Factory?*" Mort asked

brightly, as if he thought this was a wonderful suggestion. Oh, what fun!

"What are you saying?" I said to Sarah.

But Mort knew exactly what she wanted, and seeing as how making all of Sarah's dreams come true was his new *raison d'etre*, he immediately steered Lila over to Romeo's feet. "So you'll get in here."

How could he possibly have understood what she meant? Had tiny Nicolette already fallen into the pit of never-ending chocolate? I will admit, it froze me for a second. I didn't think that I would have to do anything, because surely this was the point where Lila would reach into her back pocket and pull out divorce papers. Surely she would say, When pigs fly, Mort, will I be crawling into your ex-wife's bed. But here she comes, moving gingerly across Romeo's legs as if she has some understanding of a back injury. Her face was set in resignation.

"No!" Sandy said, and grabbed her arm.

"Out!" I said, loudly this time. I pushed in next to Romeo. I felt like I was in the movie where the shark is swimming closer and closer, where the shark is pulling up onto your own tiny life raft.

Romeo's breathing was even and deep. He had no idea what he was sleeping through.

Mort got into bed down by my feet. "Seems like old times," he said to me.

"Mort, Lila, for God's sake, get out now! Romeo can't be moved around like this!"

"Look how careful I'm being," Mort said, and slid into place without creating the slightest ripple. He was not happy. No one was happy except for Sarah, who was absolutely mad with joy. She was dancing around the bed and singing both parts of a duet from the movie.

"She's lost her mind," Little Tony said.

Down on the floor by herself, Nicolette started to cry. She reached up her arms to her mother. "Up," she said. "Up."

"She can't come up," Sarah snapped. "She isn't in the movie."

"GET OUT OF MY BED!" I roared.

"Honey, wait a minute," Mort said to his youngest daughter. "Sandy, can you take the baby?"

"Get up!" Sandy screamed.

Sometimes in battle, you unexpectedly find yourself the ranking officer. You have to make a decision as to whether or not you must leave your man behind on the field in order to save him. I did not want to leave Romeo alone in that bed, but I knew I could not rid the room of this terrible plague any other way. I got up.

"Grandma!" Sarah said. "Now you have to dance with me!"

I took Sarah firmly by the arm and walked her to the hall. "Out!"

"What!" she cried. Her mouth made a perfect round 'O' of incredulity. I slammed the door.

"See this?" Mort said to Sandy. "This is exactly the sort of thing I was talking about. You don't treat a child that way. It's abusive."

I was ready to go all the way. It was time for Mort and me to enter the battle we had been skirting since the day he left me for Lila, the battle that, when it ended, would allow only one of us to live. I didn't even care if it was me. All I knew was that the world was no longer a big enough place for both of us. I jumped on him, my hands on his neck.

"Mom, no, Mom, don't!" Sandy cried.

I could feel someone pulling me from behind, then I heard Lila screaming, with Nicolette screaming behind her like a weird echo. It was a flailing ball of adults, and Little Tony was crying, "No, no!" He got ahold of Lila and Sandy got ahold of me.

"Your mother's insane!" Mort said. "Isn't this what I told you? You can't raise a child in a house like this."

"Roth?" Romeo said thickly. "Roth? Is that you?" Suddenly, the bed was bouncing so badly I was worried we had compressed yet another piece of his spine.

For a moment we were all quiet. Mort put his feet on the floor.

Little Tony ran around to the other side of the bed and picked up Romeo's hand. "It's just me, Romeo," he said in a quiet voice. "Everything's fine. Go back to sleep. I was just playing."

"Crazy kid," Romeo said, and reached up to touch Tony's head. Before his hand dropped, he was asleep again.

Nicolette was on the floor crying, and Sandy picked her up and handed her to Lila. "She needs to go downstairs," Sandy said.

Lila took her daughter in her arms and hugged her. She closed her eyes. "All of you are crazy," she said quietly.

"You didn't see *me* getting into that bed," Sandy told her, and herded her out the door.

Mort got out of the bed.

"Julie, we need to talk."

He rubbed the back of his neck. Maybe it was sore from where I had tried to strangle him. But he didn't seem to be rubbing it to make a point; he didn't seem angry at me at all, now. It was as if none of this had happened. "If we were talking about a hundred thousand, I would be completely hands off. You know that. I'm not a greedy guy. But if it's seven and a half million, that's what it is, right?"

"Get out, Mort."

"If it's seven and a half million, then I have to tell you, some of that should come to us. I'm the girl's grandfather. I'm sixty-five years old. I have a two-year-old kid."

"I know the numbers, Mort. *Out.*"

"Business has not been perfect. It's not been bust, but how is a guy my age going to make enough money to send a girl to college fifteen years from now? I might not even be around when she goes to college. Do you realize that? Lila says I've got to make provisions, and she's right, but the chances of me getting far enough ahead to put that sort of money aside at this point—well, unless I win the lottery, I don't know how it's going to happen."

Mort amazed me. He was like one of those ants that walks in a straight line. If a building is in his way, he just goes over the top of it, never around. He never loses his focus; he never hears what anyone else is saying; he just goes ahead. I could take off all my clothes and stand on my head, and he would just keep talking.

"Could we at least have this conversation in another room so we don't wake Romeo up again?" I said.

"The guy seems to be about as alert as a can of tuna fish."

"Look Mort, as far as I'm concerned, this is Sandy's decision to make. If they want to cut you in on the ticket, then *mazel tov.* I will do nothing to stand in the way. But I'm not the person you should be pleading your case to. Get out of my bed, my room, and my house. Leave me alone. I have nothing to do with this."

"Oh Jules, are you really so blind? You've got to know the way things work around here. You're the lynchpin, the compass. Nothing gets done unless you give it the okay. You've got to talk to them for me, plead my case. Otherwise, I don't stand a chance."

"Roth?" Romeo said again. "Is that Mort Roth?"

"Go back to sleep, Cacciamani. Go back to sleep in my bed."

Suddenly Romeo's eyes shot open wide as if from a terrible dream. "Julie?"

"I'm getting rid of him," I said. "It isn't easy, but I'm working on it."

Romeo reached out with one hand, his fingers clawing at the air. "Where is he?"

"What do you think," Mort said. "You're going to catch me and squeeze me to death with one hand?"

"It would work if I caught you in the right place," Romeo said.

I put my hands against Mort's shoulder and pushed, but he was a very solid sixty-five. "Let me give you some advice, Mort.

The next time you want me to do you a favor, send flowers. Write up a simple letter and stick it in a huge bouquet and send it to me. Systematically begging and insulting is never going to get you anywhere."

"Julie, get him out of here," Romeo said.

"Look at the way he talks to you," Mort said, and made a tsk, tsk noise that made me want to pull out his teeth. "I'm going downstairs. We'll talk later. I hope you're feeling better soon, Cacciamani."

"Me too, Roth. I hope I'm feeling better before you leave town."

I closed the door behind him, but there wasn't a lock. Mort himself had taken it off thirty years ago when Nora locked herself in our bedroom one night. I tried to put a chair beneath the knob the way they do in movies, but either it wasn't the right chair or it wasn't the right knob. I couldn't get it to stay.

"What in the hell just happened here?" Romeo said.

"Nothing good, and nothing that's ever going to happen again."

"I want to kill him, but I'm so sleepy . . ."

I went over and kissed Romeo's forehead. The veins were jumping out on the sides of his temples, which I didn't think could possibly be good for his health. "You've got to put this out of your mind and get some rest."

"And what about you?" he mumbled, slipping under again. "Don't you need some rest?"

"I do, but first there is a certain eight-year-old I need to kill."

❧

Luck seemed to be a key player in our house these days, running in the front door, then jumping out a window the moment you called for it. Good luck and bad luck become so intertwined that I could no longer tell where one left off and the other began. So when I came down the stairs, looking around, and Nora saw me, and said, "They're gone," I was so overcome by the good fortune of it I nearly wept.

"Sandy said no one was killed." Nora was holding her blanket up under her chin with both hands. She looked distinctly rattled.

"No one was killed *yet* would be a more accurate depiction."

"From here it sounded bad."

I nodded. "Really bad."

Sandy came in from the kitchen with both of the children. There were certain moments when Little Tony and Sandy looked so much alike it was eerie. They could line up sometimes and get exactly the same expression on their faces, which in this case was one of complete exhaustion and hollow disbelief. Sarah, on the other hand, was always a little more like her father, the elusive Sandy Anderson, who the last we heard was still riding the waves in Maui. Sarah was going to go her own way in this world.

"Sarah," Sandy said in a rasping voice. "Apologize to your grandmother."

"She threw me out of the room," Sarah said. "It was my party, and she made me leave. I didn't do anything wrong."

"Sarah—"

I held up my hand. "It's okay. The fact is, I'm not ready to accept Sarah's apology anyway, so there's no sense in forcing her to make it."

Sarah and Sandy and even Tony looked at me with complete disbelief.

I decided to level with Sarah despite her tender age. "Sarah, you've got to think about how far you can push people. I know this is an extraordinary experience you're going through, but I also know you're a better person than this. You don't have to behave so badly, even if you think you're entitled to do so."

Great, huge tears welled up in Sarah's eyes. "I was going to help everybody," she said. "I was going to do nice things, but I don't have to. All of that money is mine, and I'm going to keep all of it."

"Sarah, go to your room," Sandy said. "And do it quietly. Romeo's trying to sleep."

She turned on her heel without another word to any of us. I sat down on the edge of Nora's bed, and Sandy and Little Tony collapsed on the couch. Sandy put her arm around her son. "Come here, my neglected one," she said, and gave him a hug. "What was your name again?"

Tony giggled. It was a lovely, unfamiliar sound.

"Just how far out of hand have things gotten?" Nora asked. She was ready to make her assessment.

"She called the bank," I said. "She wanted to know how big an account she was allowed to open."

"Well, obviously she's telling people," Nora said. "Dad's here."

"She's told pretty much everybody at school," Tony said.

"What?" Sandy said. "She promised she wouldn't. Why didn't you tell us?"

Tony shrugged. "'Cause it doesn't matter. Nobody believes her. She's been taking all the kids aside one at a time during recess and making them swear they won't tell, but nobody even cares 'cause they all think she's lying. She says she's going to start coming to school in a limousine with her own driver. She says she's going to have Friday's build a restaurant in the cafeteria so everybody she likes can eat for free. She's been telling all the kids she was going to win the lottery for a long time. Now she says she won. The kids still think she's just talking."

"And what do you say when they ask you about it?"

"I tell them she's lying," Tony said.

"Smart boy," Sandy said.

"I don't see why you don't just give her the money," he said. "She'll be through with it in a week, and then everything will go back to normal."

"Do you really think your sister could spend seven and a half million in a week?" Sandy asked.

"I think she could spend it in a day," Tony said. "She's really been planning."

Sandy looked at her watch. "Well, if she's going to run through the whole windfall on Gummy Bears, I'd better get back to work. I told Plummy I was just going to drop off the kids and come straight back. She's probably going to report me to the boss."

"Can I come with you?" Tony asked. He was enjoying the light of being the good kid and didn't want to cut it short.

"Sure," Sandy said. "Bring your homework. I'll pick up some pizza for dinner on the way back."

"Mushroom and onion," Nora said. "And pineapple."

"On your half, maybe," Tony said, in a way that belied his eleven-year-old disgust.

After they were gone, Nora and I just sat there staring at each other. "It's so peaceful," I said.

Nora folded her hands across her ever-expanding stomach.

"When a woman is pregnant, especially for the first time, she should be allowed to lie in bed and have fantasies about how sweet everything's going to be. The children will make me Mother's Day cards at school, and I'll stick them to the refrigerator door with magnets. There'll be lots of kisses and walks in the park and birthday parties, that sort of thing. Being around here doesn't give a person much of an opportunity to delude herself."

"You'll get all of that," I told her. "Those are the things you hold on to when you're trying to get through the other stuff. You go back to your scrapbook and you look at those Mother's Day cards when it's two o'clock in the morning and your teenaged daughter hasn't come home."

"If I haven't apologized for that yet, I would like to do so now, officially: Mother, I am sorry for torturing you."

I got up from the end of the bed and kissed her. "Thank you," I said. "It was nothing, really."

"It's like I told Alex, for the next eighteen years we might as well just batten down the hatches and ride out the storm."

"Eighteen years?"

"Until they go to college," she said. "Until things settle down."

"Are you serious?"

"Well, I know college is going to be a fortune. Three kids, I can't even imagine it. I can only hope that one of them wants to be a plumber. We'll be working hard until they're twenty-two to make enough money."

"So you think the mothering lasts for eighteen years and the financial responsibility goes for another four after that?"

"I'm just saying the bulk of it, the thick of it. I know things will come up after that, but it isn't the same."

"How old are you, Nora?"

"I'm forty, you know that."

"And your sister?"

"So you're making a point."

"Your sister is?"

She sighed. "Thirty-six."

I picked up one of her cantaloupe-sized feet and started to rub it. She made a small sound of pure hedonistic delight. "One of you should let me know when I'm off duty," I said.

Chapter Sixteen

BEFORE I HAD ANY PERSONAL ASSOCIATION WITH winning lottery tickets, I was always stumped by the fact that winners were given an entire year to claim their prizes. Was that because the person was out of town the week of the drawing and found the ticket lying around later on? Did they then throw it in a drawer, meaning to check the winning numbers and somehow never got around to it? Or maybe the ticket got stuck in the back of a wallet, squeezed between the Mobil card and some grocery store receipts, and it languished there for more than eleven months, only to be discovered in a neatening spree.

Every now and then people wander into the lottery office moments before it closes, seeking to redeem a grand jackpot winner that was issued 364 days before. Where had they been all that time? I used to imagine they had spent the whole year madly looking for the ticket, the way I look for my glasses or keys, turning the house upside down day after day after day. But now that I was on the inside, I saw it differently. I suspected all these Johnny-come-latelies just wanted to take the extra time to say good-bye to their old life, to stave off the chaos that money always brings. They took their final year to revel in everything that was simple.

According to the rules of the Massachusetts State Lottery, a person under the age of eighteen cannot purchase a ticket and therefore cannot claim the prize. If a ticket has been purchased for a minor, a parent or legal guardian may claim the prize for that child and hold the money in trust until the child comes of age.

No one loved that idea—another ten years of Sarah compiling lists of things she wanted. Well, actually Mort loved the idea, as long as he could be the guardian. He called me on the phone to tell me he had a friend who was making a killing in high-tech stock investments, and if he could just borrow the money for say six months or a year, he could double it, keep half for himself, and give the principle seven and a half million back to Sarah untouched.

"I thought the tech boom was over," I said.

"That was the *last* tech boom. Jules, you're so behind."

The Massachusetts State Lottery also said that if more than one winning ticket was redeemed, the winners shall split the jackpot. And on a very cold morning after the big bed pileup, while the Roseman-Cacciamani household continued to dither over how to manage its good fortune, a second winner stepped forward. Or, I should say, a first winner stepped forward as we had not stepped anywhere yet. Three million, seven hundred and fifty thousand dollars gone, and not a single Barbie had been purchased yet.

When I read the news, it was so early it was still dark outside. Alex had left the paper folded, story up, for me to find. I sat in the kitchen feeling surprisingly ill. I had to keep reminding myself that what we had lost was something we never really had, that it wasn't ours to lose, and that it especially wasn't mine to lose.

"What is it?" Sandy said when she came into the kitchen. I pushed the paper over for her to see.

"Big jackpot winner in Mass Millions," she said slowly. "Jo Gottschalk of Lancaster, Ohio, brought the Mass Millions winning ticket into the Braintree office yesterday afternoon. Ms. Gottschalk is a legal secretary in the offices of . . ." Sandy put the paper down. "I guess that takes care of half our problems," she said quietly.

We sat there for a little while without saying anything, just feeling bad that we were so foolishly feeling bad. I got up and brought her a cup of coffee.

"Why do I suddenly feel so broke?" she said. "Why am I sitting here thinking, but how will we get by on 3.75 million?"

"I know what you mean. It seems like such a pathetic number."

"Belt tightening is up ahead," Sandy said.

"Good-bye, mink bedspreads."

"No private nanny for Oompah-Loompah."

"Seriously, how are we going to tell Sarah?"

Sandy folded up that piece of the paper and stuck it in her back pocket. "Well, one thing's for certain. I'm not going to tell her before she goes to school. It's going to take some time to figure out how to construct this one properly."

"Kid, you're broke. You're all washed-up."

"You know she's going to take this very, very badly."

"I wonder if we could tell her that Mort already lost half the money in the tech market," I suggested.

When Little Tony and Sarah came down for breakfast, I was already at the stove making pancakes.

"Pancakes?" Tony said. "On a Thursday? Did something bad happen?"

I turned away from the griddle, spatula in hand. Both of the children were eyeing me with deep suspicion. "Nothing bad happened," I said. "Unless you want to count yesterday. Yesterday was pretty bad. I thought it might be good for all of us to have a clean start. Pancakes are always the best thing for a clean start."

They held up their plates and were grateful. Sarah even went so far as to say, "Grandma, these are very good."

I thanked her.

After they had left for school, with Sandy throwing one last nervous look at me over her shoulder, I made a plate of pancakes for Nora and took them into the living room. "I don't want to hear a word about white flour and gluten," I said. "I saw you eating pizza last night."

"Give me the pancakes," she said.

"There's been another claim on the Mass Millions tickets. We're down to half."

Nora took a big bite of pancakes first and chewed them thoughtfully. "How is that possible? I didn't hear any screaming from the kitchen."

"We haven't told her yet. Sandy wanted to wait until after school."

"You're going to need to tell her while you're standing in a hospital emergency room. Is there any more syrup?"

I went back to the kitchen and brought out the bottle. "Just save some for Romeo."

"I looked up the game odds online." She pulled a Post-it

note off her rolling desk and held it up to me. "The chances of a perfect match were listed at 13,983,816 to one. I wonder what that would make the odds of two perfect matches?"

"Around 28 million?"

Nora shook her head. "Odds don't double. They increase exponentially. I think we're talking about some very, very big numbers."

I went back to the kitchen and fired up the stove for a third time that morning and made a batch of pancakes for Romeo. When I told him about the ticket he scarcely feigned interest.

"Maybe she'll win again later," he said philosophically. "Has Mort gone?"

"I think they're still lurking on the periphery."

"Has he come back to the house?"

"Chew your pancakes. No, he hasn't come back. You've got to put him out of your head."

"I have a lot of free time to think about things, up here. Al just brought me the unabridged *Moby-Dick* on tape. From now on, I plan either to be thinking about killing Mort or killing whales."

I took a bite of the pancakes. They were good. I had forgotten to make a plate for myself.

"Concentrate on the whales. I think Mort has pretty much

figured out that there's no money around here for him. He'll slink back to his cave soon enough."

"I still can't believe that you married him," Romeo said, with uncharacteristic grumpiness.

"Youthful folly," I said. "Nothing more than that."

It was only 9:00 A.M. when the phone rang. Nora was hard at work making the world safe for condominium complexes and Romeo was with Ishmael on the high seas and I was finishing up the last of the breakfast dishes.

"Mrs. Cacciamani?" a voice asked.

Distracted by a hundred different thoughts, I said yes.

"This is Mrs. Oates calling from Somerville Elementary. I'm calling about Sarah."

I started to say, no, you want to speak to my daughter who is really Mrs. Cacciamani, but instead I gave the only logical response I could. "Is something wrong with Sarah?"

"I'm afraid she's quite upset. We can't seem to calm her down."

Sure enough, in the background I could hear a crying that was distinctly Sarah's. "Did she tell you what was wrong?" I asked, as if I didn't know the answer.

"It seems she's been telling the children at school that she won the lottery and today several of the children told her that someone else had won. I don't know what this is all about but I think you're going to need to come over and get her, or at least talk to her until she calms down."

Poor Sarah. Who knew that there were other third-graders who followed such things? I wondered if they had told their parents and their parents in turn clipped out the article for them: "Look, Billy, that little girl Sarah must have been lying." We should have told her in her own kitchen over the safety of pancakes. Nobody wanted to get news like that in home room.

I said my good-byes and headed over to the school. Once again I found Sarah on the cot in the back office, the same damp washcloth covering her swollen eyes. This time Little Tony was sitting beside her, holding her hand.

"They let me out of class so I could stay with her until somebody got here to take her home," he told me.

"That's not our usual practice," Mrs. Oates said.

"But she was awful," Tony said. "She was screaming. Lots of the other kids in her class started to cry."

"I'm glad you were here," I said to Tony.

"Do I get to go home, too?"

I shook my head. "I don't think it works that way."

He patted his sister's hand before returning it to the cot. "Bye, Sarah. I'll see you this afternoon. Don't take any wooden nickels."

She didn't say a word. Tony shrugged and headed back to class.

"I don't think we've ever had a child go home from school because of the lottery before," Mrs. Oates said, as I once again signed the pickup papers.

I didn't tell her that Sarah had gone home from school because of the lottery before. "It's complicated," I said. "But I can assure you it won't happen again."

I scooped Sarah up and tried to thread her limp little arms into her coat. She just stared off into the middle distance with glassy despair. I led her out to the car, a little zombie, and buckled her in.

"We'll go see your mother now, would you like that?"

She leaned her forehead against the door.

"Sarah, you haven't forgotten how to speak."

"Did you know?" she said.

"Yes," I said, sorry to have to tell her the truth. "We thought it would be better to tell you after you got home from school."

And then she started to cry again.

Big Tony was working the front of the store at Roseman's, and Sandy and Plummy were in the back, putting together dazzling bouquets as fast as their nimble fingers could assemble them. When we walked through the door the little bells chimed. Tony took one look at us, and said, "Uh-oh." I had a hand on each of Sarah's shoulders for fear she would decide to experiment with fainting.

"You knew, too?" Sarah asked him.

"Um, just for a little while," Tony said. "Really just for the past hour or so."

"She had to come home from school," I said. "Somebody told her."

Sandy's face just melted, the way you do when you hear that your child is hurt. She came over and knelt in front of Sarah and took her in her arms. "I'm sorry," she said. "I know you're upset."

But Sarah pushed away from her. "Nobody told me!"

Plummy came out and stood beside the cash register. "Hi, Sarah," she said.

"Nobody told me anything! All of the kids were making fun of me. They said I'd never won. They said I was lying."

"But that isn't true," Sandy said. "You did win. You won a lot."

"Not anymore! I don't have anything anymore! I may as well never have won at all."

"I thought you still got more than three and a half million dollars," Plummy said in a puzzled voice.

"That's nothing! It's not enough. It won't be enough for me to have everything I want."

"Sarah, come on," Tony said. "That's a ton of money. That's more money than almost anybody has."

"It was all mine, and she took half, this other person. If we had just turned the ticket in at first, we'd have all the money by now and they couldn't make us give it back."

"It doesn't work that way," Sandy said.

"You don't know anything! None of you know anything! I want my money back!" Sarah picked up a bunch of mixed flowers from a bucket on the floor and started tearing their heads off and throwing them. Fistfuls of petals and leaves went shooting up through the air.

Tony and Sandy and I just stared at her. It was impossible to know what to say. I felt sorry for her, I really did, but now I was thinking it was time to reconsider corporal punishment. No one believed that the problems of parenting could be solved with a spanking anymore, but I wasn't so sure.

Then Plummy started to laugh. The redder Sarah's face became, the more viciously she attacked the flowers, the harder Plummy laughed. "Daddy, *I* want an Oompah-Loompah," she said in a strange British accent. "Get me an Oompah-Loompah *NOW*."

Sarah stopped shredding the flowers and looked up at her. "What?"

"Daddy, get me the golden ticket!" she said. Then she started laughing again.

"Why are you laughing?" Sarah said suspiciously.

"Because you're perfect!" Plummy said. "You're the perfect Veruca Salt. She was my favorite character."

Veruca Salt was the awful little rich girl who wore fur coats and ran her father ragged with her shrieking demands. To be Veruca Salt was a very, very low thing to be.

"I'm not Veruca," Sarah said slowly. "I'm Charlie Bucket."

Plummy smiled at her, a smile so generous and true that one could think that nothing but good things could come from it. "No, my darling. Charlie was a poor, generous boy who loved his family. Veruca was a smart, stylish girl who loved her money. Did you get to see all of the movie? Did I take it before you had the chance to see the whole thing?"

"No," Sarah said, puzzling hard over what she was hearing. "I saw it."

Plummy leaned over the counter and locked Sarah in with her great, dark eyes. "So tell me now, and really think about it—which one are you?"

And Sarah did think hard. She thought so hard, you could almost see her letting go of the mink bedspread and the chauffeured limousines and the Mickey Mouse waffle iron. You could almost see her reaching back for the people she loved. She dropped the few stems she was still holding and wiped her hands against her skirt. She straightened up her shoulders. "I'm Charlie Bucket," she said.

∽

Maybe all of us are connected to our better selves by a strong rope, and if we get too far away from the person we used to be, we can use that rope to pull ourselves back. It's easy to get lost in distractions, especially when you're eight, and maybe when you're eight it's also easier to find your way back to your essential goodness. After all, there isn't enough time to fall too far away from what's right.

Sarah left the flower shop that day the girl I knew before, a person who was mostly just herself and slightly modeled on the better aspects of Shirley Temple and an impoverished English boy who got a lucky break.

We held a family conference that night in the living room, with Romeo joining in on a little speakerphone that Nora plugged into her cell. And while Mort and Lila and Nicolette were not invited, they weren't left out, either. Nicolette's education was a topic of discussion. It was agreed by a unanimous vote that Alex would be in charge of operating the trust that would look after the money, and because only one person could sign the back of the ticket and claim the prize, we also agreed that that person should be Sandy.

"But Mom bought the ticket," she said. "She should have to do it."

"But then she has to gift the money to Sarah and the rest of the family, which creates another layer of taxes," Alex said. "This way it stays directly in your family."

And while it was decided that everyone on the board of the trust, which was all of us, should agree on how the money was spent, it was also agreed that Sarah, who was the owner of the ticket, should get to choose a few things she wanted without having to get anyone's okay.

Sarah closed her eyes and thought about it. She thought like Charlie Bucket. "I want my mom to have a house. I want Nicolette to go to college, and I want both of the Tonys to be doctors."

"I don't want to be a doctor," Little Tony said.

"Tough. I say you have to be."

As for Big Tony, he put his face in his hands so we wouldn't see him cry.

Then Oompah-Loompah wandered into the room and rubbed her back against Sarah's legs, and so it was decided that there should also be a very nice donation to the animal shelter where Oompah-Loompah had come from.

It took Alex a week to finish the paperwork, then on a Thursday one week before Thanksgiving, Sandy and I picked Tony and Sarah up after school so that we could all go to the Lottery headquarters in Braintree together and turn the ticket in. The kids were practically hopping up and down in the backseat.

"It isn't like we're going to walk in there and they're going to hand us all the money in a sack," Sandy explained.

"I know," Sarah said, "but it's so exciting!"

"I just need to make a quick stop at the bank," I said, and turned the car into my little branch office. Everyone piled out with me; it was too cold to wait in the car.

"Hi, Sally," I said. "I need to get back in the lockbox."

"Sure thing," she said. Sally came back with a big loop of keys. "Hey, Sarah, are you here to open up a big account?"

"Maybe later," Sarah said.

"Well, we're still waiting."

I picked up the piece of tinfoil, right on top where I'd left it, and handed it to Sandy.

"That's what you came to get?" Sarah said.

"I didn't like carrying it around."

"But it's not in there."

We all looked at Sarah, then Sandy peeled back the tinfoil. It was the top panel of a Cheerios box, cut down to the size of a lottery ticket.

"Sarah," Sandy whispered. "Where's the ticket?"

"It's in my shoe."

"You switched it?"

She nodded. "I thought it would be safer with me."

Sarah unlaced her left winter boot and produced yet another piece of tinfoil from underneath her sock.

"I'm feeling a little ill," I said slowly, and sat down in a chair at the long table used to sort through important family papers. I had locked away a Cheerios box top, while the winning ticket continued to pound the playgrounds of Somerville backed by a piece of a Kix box.

"Did anyone know the ticket was in your shoe?" Sandy asked.

Sarah shook her head.

"So all that time you were telling kids that you'd won, and they didn't believe you, you never took out the ticket and showed them?" Little Tony asked.

Sarah rolled her eyes, the last vestige of her now all-but-forgotten bad behavior. "Really," she said. "I'm not stupid."

Epilogue

KNOWING WHAT WILL HAPPEN IN THE FUTURE HAS never made the future get here any more quickly. Nora's stomach continued to rise at an alarming rate, until finally she lost the privilege of sitting up in bed and had to spend her last two months ruling her empire while flat out on her back. She said that any cervix would be incompetent when it came to holding in so much baby.

She valiantly managed to keep them with her until two weeks into her seventh month, at which time she gave birth to two girls and a boy, all of whom were healthy and tiny. They named one of the girls Ella for my mother, and another girl Rose for Alex's grandmother, and the boy they called Charlie for no reason at all. Nora said she'd just gotten used to hearing the name.

She came home a full month before the babies, who slept in

warm plastic incubators back at the hospital until they grew to more respectable sizes. In that month Nora spent her days at the hospital, but at night she and Alex kept coming back to our house to sleep in the hospital bed that was still in the living room. I never asked why, nor did I ask if she planned to bring the babies back to live with me as well.

They were so cute, those babies, and as crazy as it would have been, I would have given it a try. I was finally discovering what Nora would know someday herself: Your children leave soon enough, and all the time you have them around you is actually a wonderful thing.

Tony and Sandy and Little Tony and Sarah found a house that was halfway between my house and Romeo's in Somerville, and on the day they finally left, which was the same week that Nora and Alex and the rental bed had gone, I stood in the driveway and cried.

Tony was working on his applications to medical school, Sandy had become the star florist after Plummy's return to New York, Sarah had taken up the cello, and Little Tony, after many questions and badgering, finally admitted that what he'd really like to have were tap-dancing lessons. I still see them almost every day, but it isn't the same as running into them in the kitchen in the middle of the night, which is a good thing and a sad thing, too.

As for Romeo, in the time that it took him to finish *Moby-Dick* he made a full recovery. One day I came home from the flower shop (I had started going back for a couple of hours in the afternoon) and found Romeo sitting in the armchair, dressed and reading the newspaper. All of his belongings, which had slowly migrated over to my house these past months, were folded neatly into three paper bags, which were sitting by the door.

"I'm ready," he said.

"Ready for what?" I asked, but it was only a hopeless stall on my part. I knew what he meant. I also knew that I wasn't ready at all.

He put his hands on his thighs with a light slap and stood up. It was so elegant and effortless a gesture, anyone would have thought he was a man who stood up by himself all the time.

"I'm ready to face the stairs. Dominic came by today and gave me a clean bill of health. He says I've been loitering, actually. He thinks I could have gone a long time ago."

"But what did Al say?" I always knew the priest was on my side.

"Al said it was about time I started making you sandwiches for a change."

I closed my eyes, hoping to keep back the big tears that were welling up there, but eyelids can only do so much.

"Hey," he said, and came and put his arms around me. "Are these tears of joy?"

I shook my head. "I just didn't think it would be today," I said.

Romeo kissed one eye and then the other, then he took my hand and led me to the top of the staircase. "Sarah's not down there waiting for me, is she?"

"Nobody's home at all," I said miserably. Wasn't this all I had ever wanted: A place of my own? A little quiet? Every step we took felt like a foot placed exactly on top of my heart.

But Romeo didn't hesitate a bit. In fact, it all seemed so easy for him that I suspected something was up. "You've been down here before, haven't you?"

He smiled and squeezed my hand. "I practiced a little bit on my own. I didn't want to be a nervous wreck in front of you when it was time to go."

I wiped my eyes with my free hand. "It would have been a little bit easier if we'd both been wrecks together."

When we got to the foot of the stairs, Romeo kissed me. "You've been as good to me as any one person could ever be to another person."

I hugged him, careful not to press too hard. "You're easy to be nice to."

He kissed me again, then stopped and looked up the stairs.

"One minute. I forgot my stuff." And with that he shot right back up again and came down holding all three of his bags, not needing me or the banister at all.

It was then that I realized Romeo had waited as long to go as he possibly could, as a way of helping me. I drove him the ten blocks back to his house, but I didn't go inside. I just waved and blew him a kiss. Then I cried all the way home.

Everyone had predicted that Romeo would get better, that sooner or later he would get back his strength and leave the nest. I knew as I walked from empty room to empty room that what had happened was only right and natural, even if that knowledge brought me no comfort whatsoever. I tried to make myself a nice dinner, but I couldn't eat it. I tried to read a few pages of *Moby-Dick,* but I couldn't concentrate.

The only thing that could have brought me any comfort from missing Romeo was Romeo himself, but I didn't want to call him. He deserved to have a little time with his family. After all, we had been together almost every minute of every day since he hurt his back, and I could certainly wait until tomorrow to talk to him, the very thought of which set me off crying again.

When I dried my eyes, I took to staring at the phone like a lonesome teenaged girl. Because I was staring at the phone, I didn't see him coming up the back steps. He tapped on the glass, and I gave a small shriek.

"I didn't meant to scare you," he said once I let him inside.

It had been weeks, months, years since he left, I had never been so glad to see anyone. "I was waiting by the phone."

"And now it turns out you should have been waiting by the door."

He kissed me, and I pressed my face against his cold neck.

"Did you forget something?" I said hopefully.

"You could say that."

"Do you want your copy of *Moby-Dick* back? I haven't finished it yet."

Romeo shook his head. "I was there in my house with my mom and my kids, and when I went upstairs to go to bed I thought, this isn't my room."

"That's strange." I pulled out a chair for him, and we sat at the breakfast table with our knees touching. My heart was beating like a hummingbird in double time.

"I've been sleeping in that room for almost forty years, but when I went back there tonight, I don't know." He shook his head. "It was all over."

"So you're looking for a place to stay?"

Romeo nodded and pulled out his wallet. "I went by the CVS on my way over." He took out a slip of paper and put it on the table between us. "I bought us a lottery ticket."

I picked it up and looked at it. It looked exactly like Sarah's ticket, just a tiny white slip of paper. "Nobody wins twice," I said, but I didn't believe it.

Romeo took my hand and pressed it against his cheek. Never was I so glad or so grateful for anything. There were not enough winning tickets in the world to come anywhere close to this. I closed my eyes so that I could remember everything exactly the way it was, right at that moment at my own kitchen table. Romeo had come back. It was the happiest moment of my life.

When I opened my eyes, I was wearing a ring.

"Romeo?"

"It was really late," he said. "CVS was the only place that was open."

The ring was very sparkly and not so big that it couldn't be believable. Besides, I didn't have my glasses on. I gave the band a squeeze until I had adjusted it to my size. A little hiccup of a cry caught in my throat. Zsa Zsa Gabor had never had a ring as fine as this. "It's beautiful."

"You can't just buy a ring at CVS, you know. It was a free gift. I had to buy three tubes of lipstick to get it." He reached into his pocket and put three blue shiny tubes down on the table. "I wasn't sure which color you'd like."

"I'll wear them all," I said. I wagged my fingers to make the light in the little stone dance. "Do you really want to get married?"

Romeo shrugged. "I feel like we're already married. We can get married or we can have a long engagement. We can do anything you'd like. I just want you to know—" His voice broke off and he shook his head. "There's nobody for me but you," he said finally.

I handed him a tissue from the box I was working my way through. Then Romeo and I started to kiss, a kiss not unlike the one that had gotten us into so much trouble in the first place.

"I'm experiencing déjà vu," I said.

"We were on our way upstairs," he said.

"That's right," I said. "But this time I'm carrying you."

He laughed, and we made our way up the stairs together, equal and side by side, dropping our clothes like a trail of bread crumbs, just in case we ever decided to go back down again someday.

༄

From that day forward, Romeo would go to the store and work on arrangements, go and see his mother in the evenings, read to her and get her settled into bed at night, and when everything was finished, he would always come back to me. Lucky me. The house was too huge and too empty for one person.

Even Oompah-Loompah was gone. I was, as I had always been these past three years, extremely grateful for Romeo.

The lottery ticket Romeo bought for me didn't win, but I kept it anyway as a reminder of what it means to get lucky. As for Sarah's ticket, it took forever to get the money. Sandy and Tony took out a bank loan for the down payment on the house while they waited for the Great State of Massachusetts to pay up. A major investigation was launched after it was discovered that certain lottery tickets might be fakes. The one that had spent such a long time in Sarah's shoe was fine, but the one that was turned in by Ms. Jo Gottschalk of Lancaster, Ohio, had never been real at all—which meant that an eight-year-old who had found a way to cut back to three million, seven hundred and fifty thousand dollars was restored to her full seven and a half million. Sarah said she wanted to send us on vacation. We're still waiting to hear the decision of the board.